FINDING YOU

DL GALLIE

Proofread by **Victoria** at **Cruel Ink Editing** and **Margaret Neal**

Formatting and interior design by **DL Gallie**

As an editor in the cutthroat world of publishing, books are my life.

Like in the romance novels I edit, I always dreamed of a sexy billionaire swooping in and wooing me.

Then, one evening, I met a gorgeous man in a bar.

It was only meant to be one night of passion, but one turned into two. Then, a few weeks later, fate intervened in the most unlikely of places.

Like that first night, we kept each other warm, but come morning, I snuck out.

Imagine my surprise when I land my dream job at Blackstone Publishing and I meet the CEO, Bastian—*Oh my God, I slept with my new boss … twice*—Blackstone. As much as I try to leave him in my memories, I'm finding it harder and harder to ignore his advances.

Eventually, I give in, and it's everything I wanted—until two pink lines and a disgruntled ex-employee turn my world upside down.

It seems that happily-ever-afters might only happen in the books I edit.

For the members of DL's Liquor Cabinet
Thanks for a great playlist and for all the support.
You guys are amazing—this one is for you.

1

———

BASTIAN

"You're fired, Chad," my head of Human Resources, Kerrie, says to my editorial director, well, ex-editorial director, Chad Hastings. Here at Blackstone Publishing, we have a nonfraternization policy, and it turns out Chad's been screwing one of our interns, Mara Mara—yes, that's the intern's name—for weeks now. Security caught them on camera, and the proof is irrefutable. We looked into things further, and it looks like he's been breaking the policy for years now. Therefore, Kerrie and I had no choice, we had to fire him and Mara Mara for misconduct.

"Fuck you, this is bullshit," Chad shouts. His nostrils flaring and the vein in his forehead throbbing.

"Watch your mouth," I warn him.

"Like you have a fucking leg to stand on, Mr. 'Fucks Anything with a Vagina.' You think 'cause you're the billionaire CEO, the rules don't apply to you."

"Not that my personal life is any of your concern, but I have never slept with an employee of mine. I never mix business with pleasure. Never have and never will." And that's a statement I stand by. Yes, I enjoy the company of different women most nights, but the women I bed have never been employed at Blackstone Publishing. Mixing business and pleasure is never a good idea, and when I started this company, I made a vow to follow that policy. All these years later, I can say that I've stuck to my guns. Don't get me wrong, I've been tempted from time to time, but I hold myself to the same rules as every other person in this building. I'd be a hypocrite if I didn't.

"Like fuck you haven't," he says, his lip curling into a sneer.

Chad is not happy that he and Mara have been let go, but rules are rules. "I've heard how all the chicks here gush over you. Hell, even Simon in accounting thinks you're hot."

"Admiring someone for their looks is one thing, but breaking company policy and sleeping with a fellow employee is another. You not only slept with a colleague, but you also did it on the premises." He glares at me. "Would you like to see the video evidence I have of you and Ms. Mara fucking all over the building? The least you could have done was not do it at the office."

"This is fucking bullshit," he growls again.

"Whether you think that or not," Kerrie interjects, "when you started here, you signed your contract, which explicitly laid out the nonfraternization policy."

"No one reads that shit," he protests.

"Well then, that's on you, Chad," I say, deadpan. "Security will escort you to your office, and you have one hour to clear your things. Kerrie will finalize your last check, and by the close of business today, you will have been paid all that you are entitled to." Chad just sits there, shaking his head. "I'm sorry it's come to this, Chad. You are a fine editor, but you broke the rules."

"Fuck this and fuck you," he growls, smashing his hands down onto the conference room table. Pushing himself upright, he shoves his chair back, causing it to crash into the wall behind him. Without another word, he storms out of the room, slamming the door on his way out.

"Well, that went well," Kerrie says, dropping her pen and shaking her head.

"It went better than I expected, and I'm sorry you had to do this."

She laughs. "Bas, I'm the head of HR. It's my job."

"Nonetheless, I'm sorry."

"To be honest, I'm glad he's gone. He might have been a good editorial director, but he's a deplorable human being."

"What do you mean?" I ask, shock flows through

me at this revelation. Chad has always been friendly around me, but then again, I was his boss.

"The way he used to speak to people always pushed the boundaries in my eyes, but he never crossed a line that would hold up in court. Therefore, from an HR perspective, I couldn't do anything about it."

Sitting here, I stare at my HR manger, shocked that this was going on under my nose. I pride myself on a safe and respectful workplace. The fact that I never knew or saw anything like this occurring doesn't sit well with me. Silently, I make a vow to be more present. Just because I'm the owner doesn't mean I can sit in my ivory tower while my minions do all the hard work.

"Well, he's gone now."

"That he is. I'll start looking for a replacement, but in the meantime, I think Lainey can step in."

Kerrie's suggestion is good but I have a better idea, and something that we probably should have done in the first place. "How about we promote Lainey to editorial director, and we hire a new editor? She was my second choice when I promoted Chad, and in hindsight, I should have gone with her."

"They were both excellent candidates, Bas. It was a hard choice to decide between the two of them, but in the end, Chad had more experience, even though Lainey has a killer personality and bakes the best savory muffins."

"I should have listened to you," I tell her, and my mouth waters as I think about Lainey's muffins.

"Can I get that in writing?" she playfully teases me.

"Hardy har har," I throw back at her. "Are you okay to deal with Mara Mara, or do you need me to be there for that?"

She shakes her head. "I've got this."

"You're the best. What would I do without you?"

"I'm sure you'd be fine, but remember this conversation when bonus time comes around."

Laughing at her, we pack up our things, and as Kerrie and I are walking out of the conference room, I see Chad being escorted out by two security guards. He looks up, and our gazes catch. If looks could kill, I'd be dead. Then, like a mature adult, he flips me the bird just as the elevator door shuts.

After heading back to my office, I drop into my chair. Thank fuck I'm meeting my brother, Beau, for drinks this afternoon. This has been a shit week, and it's only Wednesday. I could really use a drink ... and a quick fuck.

Beau is my younger brother, and he's a lawyer at Blackstone, Neal, and Barber. Beau may be my brother, but he's also my best friend. He and I are two peas in a pod. We were born only one year apart, almost to the day. Growing up, most people thought we were twins. Wherever he went, I went. The only time we were apart was for college. I stayed here and went to business school, and he went to Harvard and studied law.

When I finished my degree, I started Blackstone Publishing, and when he finished law school, he returned home and started his firm with two guys he met at Harvard.

Even with our busy schedules, Beau and I always catch up at least once a week, and when time prevails, we head up to Lake Geneva for a guys' weekend.

The day is finally over, thank-fucking-God.

After packing up, I head over to Bin 501 to meet up with Beau. When I step inside, I'm surprised at how busy it is for a Wednesday night. It's packed. We've been coming to Bin 501 for as long as I can remember, and the owner, Branson, has since become a good friend of ours. The bar is located just around the corner from both our offices, and they have the best whiskey range—for a wine bar.

"Your round, Bas," Beau hollers when I join him at the high-top table in the back.

We do the bro one-arm / back slap hug before I remove my coat. There's still a chill in the air, but spring is right around the corner. I cannot wait to say goodbye to winter, I'm over the sludge and cold. Give me the heat of summer and the beach anytime. Weather in Chicago is unpredictable, and knowing my luck, we'll get seven inches of snow next week because I just jinxed it by thinking about summer.

"Why's it my round?" I question my brother, who is smiling brightly. "Shouldn't it be *yours* since we're celebrating *your* divorce from Volderwhore."

"And *that* is why it's your round. My ass is broke now."

Beau and Kirby should never have gotten married, but he was "in love" and couldn't live without her. While he was smitten with her as a person—God only knows why, because she's the vapidest person I've ever met. Turns out, Kirby was only smitten with his bank account. One weekend, Beau found her with the gardener at their Lake Geneva home, and he left her. Turns out, she was also getting it on with the doorman of their building ... and the delivery boy ... and the housekeeper. Yep, Kirby didn't discriminate when it came to screwing my brother over.

You'd think that, since he's a top-notch lawyer, he would have had an ironclad prenuptial agreement, but nope, my dear brother, did not. This allowed the bitch to make the divorce as difficult as possible. Finally, after seven long months, they reached an agreement, and as of two forty-three this afternoon, he's a single man. Volderwhore is no longer a Blackstone—not that she ever took our last name.

In the proceedings, he lost the Lake Geneva home and his car, a Maserati Granturismo. He was sad to lose his car, but as I reminded him, that one had memories of Kirby all over it ... literally. Those two would fuck like rabbits, and they wouldn't care if they were in public or not. I don't know how many times I caught them in the parking garage because they couldn't wait until they got to their apartment. In regard to the lake house, again, he wasn't too concerned since it was the place where his life fell apart.

The one thing he refused to give up? His apartment. After winning his first big case, he bought himself a luxury apartment and since it was his before they got married, it wasn't considered a joint asset, therefore she had no claim to it.

How we never knew she was a lying, scheming, cheating whore, I will never know.

After the discovery of the many, many people she was sleeping with, Beau asked for a favor, and as the now owner of his building—perks of being a billionaire —I was more than happy to comply. I had the doorman and the concierge fired for screwing over my brother. Then, we changed the locks and had her banned from the building. The day she tried to gain access, I just so happened to be returning from work, and it was priceless to see her being forcibly removed from the building.

"Fine, first round's on me," I agree, but even if he

hadn't asked, I would have done it. I mean, it's not every day your brother finalizes his divorce.

"Not like you can't afford it," he throws at me. Flipping him the bird, I make my way to the bar. Waiting my turn, I smile when I see Suzanne is working tonight.

"Mr. B," she says in greeting when it's my turn.

And like usual, her cheeks darken, and I know she's thinking about what I'm thinking about. A few years ago, Beau and I tag-teamed her one night. I thought it would be awkward with her after that night, but things have remained professional, well, as professional as it can get between a barmaid and a patron. But to this day, she still blushes and I'm not gonna lie, it's good for the ego. Nothing will ever eventuate between us. Don't get me wrong, she's a great girl with a killer rack, but she and I weren't compatible between the sheets. She and Beau had an explosive connection and I spent most of our night with her watching from the sidelines. That night was like my very own live-action porno, and I'm man enough to admit that, from time to time, I've used memories of the occasion to get myself off. Another tick in the compatibility box between Beau and Suzanne, she's also studying law and has been doing some intern work at his firm.

"The usual?" she asks, snapping my attention back to the present.

"Not tonight. Two glasses of champagne, please." A chuckle escapes me at my order. Beau will be expecting whiskey, but since we're celebrating, bubbly stuff it is.

"Celebrating?"

"Yep." I nod. "Beau is finally divorced from Volderwhore." Suzanne's demeanor changes at that piece of news, and I can't help but chuckle to myself. She straightens up and, not-so-subtly, glances behind me, looking for my brother. I know the moment she spots him, because her killer smile widens. It morphs from her "customer service" smile to her "I'm genuinely happy to see you" smile. I've had my suspicions she's had a crush on him since that night, but soon after, he met Volderwhore and we all know how that turned out. But now he's a free agent, I'm going to push him to pursue something with her. Seems my highest-selling genre is starting to rub off on me, what with me wanting to play matchmaker and all.

"On me," she says, placing the flutes down in front of me. "And pass on my congratulations to Beau."

"Will do, and thanks." I pop a twenty on the bar for a tip. She nods and pockets the bill before getting back to work.

Walking back over to my brother, I place his drink before him. Smirking when he scrunches his brow at my drink choice. Raising my glass for a toast, I see the moment it clicks as to why I got the bubbly. "To single life." He taps his glass against mine and repeats the toast. "Ohhh, and Suzanne passes on her congratulations."

"Suzanne's here?" He perks up at that tidbit of information, and I smile to myself. I'm glad to see my brother happy again. He's been on pussy hiatus while dealing with the divorce, but that's all in the past now. It's time for him to get laid again. If anyone deserves happiness, it's him.

2

AUDREY

IF ONE MORE GUY HITS ON me tonight, I'm going to stab him in the eye with my pen. Then, I'm going to stomp on his balls with my stiletto heels. Can't a girl just sit at a bar and enjoy her dirty martini while she reads the spicy manuscript in front of her? FYI, the answer is no, well, not tonight anyway.

Loser number ... I've lost count ... suddenly snaps his gaze away from me, and when I follow his line of sight, I shake my head. The barmaid has bent down to grab a bottle of wine from the lower fridge, and as she does, her short black skirt rides up, almost baring her ass for all to see. She pulls it back down as she stands up, and the creep next to me licks his lips.

He winks, well, I think he's winking but he could also be having a fit, what do I know? I'm not a doctor. "What time do you get off, sweet cheeks?" he calls out like the desperate loser he is.

"Never," she grumbles as she pours two glasses of wine and hands them to the gentleman waiting. He tells her to keep the change and walks off. She rings up his drinks and pops the change into her apron.

She glances down the bar for someone new to serve, but the only person waiting is the jerk next to me. Reluctantly, she looks at him. "What can I get you?" Her tone has no emotion, but she politely offers him a small smile because she obviously needs the tips.

"Dang, girl, your smile just took my breath away."

He seriously did not just use that line. I'm shaking my head at his desperation, but from the look on her face, she's about to have some fun, and I'm here for it. Dropping my pen, I pick my drink up and settle in for the show.

She rests her palms on the edge of the bar, leans on her hands, and stares intently at him. The douche next to me drops his gaze to her chest, and again, licks his lips. He's oblivious to the look of disdain on the barmaid's face. This is like a car wreck, and I can't look away. In slow motion, she leans in and beckons him closer. The clueless guy rests his arms on the bar top and pushes himself forward, hoping to get closer to the waitress. There's about an inch separating them. She flutters her lashes and murmurs, "And your breath is pushing me away. Now, order a drink or you can show yourself to the door."

"Fucking bitch," he huffs out. Pushing off the bar,

he storms off with his tail tucked between his legs—and no drink.

"You're my new hero," I tell her.

"I've heard them all, and I have a comeback for each and every one of the slimeballs who come in here."

"I bet you do."

"Another?" she asks, nodding to my nearly empty drink.

"Please."

She goes about making my dirty martini, and I turn my attention back to the manuscript before me. A new drink is placed in front of me, and I pick up the glass. Taking a sip, I close my eyes and savor the flavor as it dances over my taste buds.

Picking up the toothpick, I bite one of the olives and chew. Then, I feel a presence beside me. *Not again*, I think to myself. I'm about to give him a piece of my mind about personal space when a deep, masculine voice drawls, "Whiskey, neat."

The barmaid's cheeks darken, and her reaction garners my attention. She nods and timidly says, "Coming up." Her voice is shaky, and now I'm really intrigued.

Sitting here, I watch as she turns, reaches up, and grabs the whiskey from the top shelf. Her skirt is riding up again, but the man next to me doesn't notice, because he's looking at me.

He's.

Looking.

At.

Me.

Why is he looking at me and not her ass? The ass before us is spectacular in that skirt. I'm woman enough to appreciate a fine ass on another female. The same goes for tits and looks. She pours him his drink and places it on the bar, a slight shake to her hand.

Her reaction to this man is intriguing. She's played it cool all night, but this man unsettles her, therefore, I need to play it cool with him. Picking up my glass, I take a sip, subtly lift my gaze to the side, and my breath hitches in my throat.

Beside me is the sexiest man I have ever seen. Dark hair. A chiseled jaw with a slight scruff. Plump lips and the bluest of blue eyes. And right now, said blue eyes are currently boring into me.

"Evening," he utters. Lifting the tumbler to his lips, he takes a sip, never taking his eyes off of me.

Sitting here, I watch his Adam's apple bob as he swallows the amber liquid. My brain clicks into gear. He said hello, and I'm currently being rude just staring at him. "Evening," I return, but I don't focus on him. I focus on my drink. I need a moment to calm my erratically beating heart. If not for my rib cage, it would be beating out of my chest, Bugs Bunny-style.

Taking another sip of my cocktail, the liquid soothes me, and I finish the rest of my drink. Placing the empty glass beside my manuscript, I grab my napkin to wipe my lips, just as the man commands, "And another for the lady, please, Suzanne."

"I'm fine," I refute, covering my glass and shaking my head toward the bartender. She looks between me and the man beside me, as if sensing something brewing. She grabs my empty glass and walks away, leaving me alone with this mystery man. Lifting my gaze to his, I add, "I've already had two."

"Join me for dinner?"

"That's awfully forward of you. What if I were waiting for my husband?"

"You're not," he arrogantly states. His gaze bores into mine.

"Or my wife?"

"You're not," he brazenly replies.

"And what makes you so sure?"

"There's no ring on your finger—"

"Maybe I just don't wear one ... or I lost it."

"You don't have a tan line, therefore, you didn't lose it. And if you were mine, you'd be wearing a wedding ring to show all the other assholes out there that you're taken. Also, I wouldn't leave you alone for a second."

"I'm not a possession for you to piss on."

"Urophilia is not my thing."

"Not the point I was making."

"Your point is moot, now, me. You. Dinner."

He's an assertive man, I'll give him that, but I'm no

pushover. Spinning in my chair, my leg brushes against his thigh, and with a quick shuffle, he's standing between my legs. If I move again, he will know he's affecting me, and I refuse to give him the upper hand. The barmaid places another drink down and and winks at me, before serving another customer. The gentleman, now between my thighs, picks it up and hands it to me.

Our fingers brush ever so briefly, and a jolt of electricity zaps from him to me. My panties dampen from the brief contact, and now I'm imagining what would happen if he were to slide his hand up my thigh, push my panties to the side, and finger fuck me. I'll tell you what would happen, I'd soak his fingers with my arousal. I've never had such a visceral reaction to a man before, but then again, I've never met a man who looks like him before. He's like a book boyfriend but in the flesh.

Lifting my drink up, I salute him and take a sip. Normally, I'd walk away and not look back, but not only does he have me trapped, there's something about him that makes me powerless to say no. My head begins to nod on its own to his dinner invitation. *Dammit, Audrey,* I internally berate myself at how easily I fell for his charm.

"Excellent," he croons, smiling at me. The small lip lift is enough to disintegrate my panties. This man is hot, but when he smiles, he's downright attractive. Words elude me.

"Let's finish our drinks, and then we can get out of here ..."

He's waiting for my name. I never give out my real name, so I give him my nickname. "Drey. And you are?"

"Bastian, but my friends call me Bas." He offers me his hand.

My breath hitches when I place my palm in his, and another spark jolts between us. This one is much more powerful, and this time, the spark heads straight to my traitorous vagina and my already soaked panties.

As I sit here, sipping on my drink, I wonder if I should throw caution to the wind and just go for it. Have a little fun. I mean, what's the worst that could happen?

3

———

BASTIAN

WAITING for this mysteriously sexy woman to say yes to my dinner invitation is torture.

Pure torture.

After what feels like an eternity and a day, she nods. That slight movement made my day even better. "Excellent," I confirm. "Let's finish our drinks and then we can get out of here ..." *Shit, I don't even know this beautiful woman's name.* I leave my sentence hanging and thankfully, she puts me out of my misery.

"Drey. And you are?"

"Bastian, but my friends call me Bas."

Offering her my hand, she gently places hers in mine and we shake. Her breath hitches, and I know she felt it, too. I've never felt a connection with a woman like this before, physically or metaphorically. Even though she's sitting down, I can tell she's a knockout. She has this aura about her that shines brightly. Her wavy blonde hair is what first caught my attention, it shimmered in the dark lighting of the bar. Almost like a beacon in the dark of night calling to me.

She was chatting with Suzanne like she didn't have a care in the world, sipping on her martini and thwarting off the advances of all the men around her. Even from where I was sitting with Beau, I knew she was a ballbuster. Case in point—our interaction before she accepted my dinner invitation.

Throwing back the rest of the whiskey in my glass, I place the empty tumbler down on the bar top. "I just need to say goodbye to my brother, and then we can go."

"And I need to finish my drink."

"You drink up, and I'll be right back," I tell her. Quickly, I make my way back over to Beau. "I have a—"

"You dirty dog, you," he interrupts, teasing me, but the grin on his face gives him away. Then, I notice his gaze has drifted to the bar and a certain waitress.

"Dude, just man up and ask Suzanne out. I mean, there's nothing holding you back now." He looks at me, shock written all over his face. "And don't even try and say 'but the two of us have fucked her' because that point is moot. You and I both know I was nothing but a bystander that night. Yes, my dick may have entered her vagina, but it was you who made her come. And it was my hand that made me come because watching the two of you together was the hottest porno I've ever seen

... even if seeing my brother's orgasm face is kind of creepy."

"Fuck off, you loved every creepy minute." He waggles his eyebrows and a chuckle escapes me. Then he looks steadfastly at me. "You really think I have a chance?"

"I know you have a chance. Now, get over to the bar and ask her out."

"What about you?"

"I'll be fine because I have a dinner date with a smoking hot blonde, and I'm hoping to have pussy for dessert."

"You're a foul-mouthed human being ... and I'm proud to call you my brother and friend."

"Back at ya, buddy. Now, go get the girl."

"You too, Brother, you too."

We say our goodbyes, and I head back to the bar, but I pause mid-step because the seat where Drey was sitting is now empty. Her martini sits untouched, and her bag is gone.

"She left," I mumble, completely stunned. No woman has ever done that to me before. Shaking my head—and not in the mood to people anymore—I walk outside and text my driver to come collect me and take me home.

While I wait, I think over my interaction with this Drey woman. We only spoke briefly, but she's weaved her web and ensnared me. I'm intrigued and pissed off that she took off like that. Little does she know, I'm the king of games, and she has just thrown down the gauntlet. She will be mine.

Climbing into the car when Hector arrives, I rest my head against the seat as he pulls back into traffic. Staring out the window, I watch the city pass by. Tonight is not ending how I imagined it would, and it's left me in a sour, surly mood.

I say good night to Hector as we arrive at my building, I exit the car and head inside. Nodding at the night staff, I climb into the elevator and it whisks me up to my penthouse. Leaning against the wall, I mumble to myself, "Finding you is now on the top of my agenda."

Three nights later, Suzanne says, "Back again," when I walk into Bin 501 and take a seat at the bar. Once again, a cheeky grin appears on her face. Ever since my encounter with Drey the other night, I've been back, hoping to see her, but I've had no luck. Had Suzanne not been teasing me about the one who got away, I would have thought I'd made up the blonde-haired goddess.

"Yep," I reply, letting the 'P' pop.

Today was epically unproductive, all I did was think about Drey and her seductive green eyes. I haven't been able to stop thinking about her since I saw her three nights ago, but today, the thoughts ramped up, and just before lunch, I was close to going into my personal bathroom and rubbing one out. *What am I a horny fifteen-year-old boy?* All I could think about was all the dirty, sexy things I'd like to do to her as punishment for leaving me the other night.

Speaking of the other night, when I arrived home after she left me high and dry, I went into the shower and jacked off like the horny teenager I've since become. Mental images of Drey on her knees clouded my mind. It wasn't enough to sate me, and I've been a fucking grump ever since.

Kerrie told me I needed to get laid as we finalized the advertisement for Lainey's replacement. Lainey was over the moon when we offered her Chad's job, and in one day, she's achieved more than he did in the entirety of last month. I definitely should have given her the job in the first place, but hindsight is a bitch.

"Bas, how's it going?" Branson asks as he steps behind the bar.

"I'm good. And you?"

"Can't complain."

"I hear you're a dad, again."

"That I am. Sadie and Sasha are gorgeous, and KJ is a great big brother to his baby sisters." A smile graces my face as I listen to my buddy talk about his family. It's so great to see him happy. A few years back, his life was turned upside down when his brother, Kody, and KJ's bio dad, died suddenly. Fate stepped in, and

Kasey, his now wife and his dead brother's fiancée, got her second chance at love. It sounds worse than it is, but if you ask me, it's a beautiful story of a second chance at love.

Shaking my head, I smirk to myself because once again, my romance department is making me all mushy and shit. "What are you doing here on a school night?" he asks me when he's finished telling me all about his new twins.

"Just having a drink," I say, earning myself a scoff disguised as a sneeze from Suzanne.

Branson flicks his gaze from me to Suzanne. "I feel like I'm missing something?"

"You're not," I tell him, giving Suzanne the evil eye.

"So, you don't want to know that she-who-shall-not-be-named is in a booth in the back?"

"She is?" I quickly ask, my tone three octaves higher than usual and my heart is rapidly beating, threatening to burst through my rib cage.

"Back left corner." She nods in the direction, and when I look to where she indicated, I see Drey sitting there, looking as gorgeous as ever with a pen between her lips. She's wearing glasses that are giving off sexy librarian vibes, and once again, she's focused on what she's reading. Her blonde locks are on top of her head in a messy bun, and in front of her is a martini—an almost empty martini.

Looking back to Suzanne, she nods before I even ask. "On it."

Before she makes Drey's drink, she hands me mine—did I mention I love this place? Without another word, she gets to work making another cocktail for Drey.

"Do I even want to know?" Branson asks.

"Nothing to tell ... yet."

He shakes his head and chuckles. "And on that note, I'm out. It was good to see you again, Bas."

Branson steps out from behind the bar, slaps me on the back, and walks out. A few moments later, Suzanne places a fresh cocktail in front of me and winks before she walks away.

Picking up both drinks, I walk across the bar. Placing the drink down next to the now-empty glass on Drey's table, I slide into the booth across from her. "We meet again," I say in place of a hello.

"Are you stalking me?"

"If I were stalking you, I would have found you three nights ago." She throws her head back and laughs. "I still owe you dinner."

"I've already eaten," she says, grabbing the olive from her empty glass and popping it into her mouth.

"You need to eat more than olives."

"And why do I need to eat more than olives?"

"Because you are going to need your stamina for what I have planned for you."

"And who says I have plans with you?"

This woman is something else. Women usually fall at my feet. Begging for me to devour them. That's not me being cocky, it's a fact. Not to toot my own horn, but I have the looks, the dick, and the actions to back it all up. Porn stars could learn a thing or two from me about what can be done in the bedroom.

Before I leave a woman in bed, she's left completely sated and ruined for the next man to bed her.

"I do believe you agreed to have dinner with me the other night. But you pulled a Cinderella, and instead of leaving behind a glass slipper, you left a full martini. That in itself is reason for you to have dinner with me, because Suzanne makes a killer martini, and you let one go to waste."

"I'll be sure to pass on my apologies to her later."

"You can apologize on our way out."

"I'm not leaving here to have dinner with you."

"I never said we were leaving here to go have dinner. I just said you *will* be leaving here with me."

"I never agreed to leave here with you. Who made that decision?" She leans forward and rests her elbows on the table. The movement pushes her tits together, and my gaze drops briefly before I look back into her eyes.

Leaning back into the booth, I outstretch my arm along the top of the red velvet chair. "I did," I tell her matter-of-factly. "You may have gotten away once,

Drey, but I will not be leaving this place without you tonight."

4

AUDREY

"Is that so, Bastian?"

"You remembered my name." He seems genuinely shocked by me remembering his name. I would have thought a cocky bastard like him would be gloating.

"It was easy to because *The NeverEnding Story* was my favorite movie as a kid."

"Well, Audrey, I'm flattered. So—"

"Hold up," she interrupts me. "How do you know my name is Audrey?" I'm positive, when we met the other day, I went with my nickname, Drey. I never give my real name when a guy hits on me—stranger danger and all that—but it seems Bastian is either a mind reader, or maybe even a stalker ... since he found me here at Bin 501 again. Recently, I moved into a building just around the corner, and one afternoon when I was walking home, I happened to glance up and the sign caught my eye, so I went inside, and I found my new happy place. And the bartenders here just so happen to make the best martini I have ever had. No matter who is on, they are always amazing.

"Well, you don't look like a Drey."

"And what does a Drey look like?" He nonchalantly shrugs at me.

"As I was saying, you don't look like a Drey, so I went with Audrey since Audrey Hepburn is the leading lady in my favorite movie."

"*Breakfast at Tiffany's* is your favorite movie?" He nods. "Really?"

"Yep, so shall—"

"And you went with Audrey. Why not Andrea?"

He ponders my question for a moment. "The name Audrey was calling to me, and now, it seems I have another favorite Audrey. Since we're connected by favorites, we *must* have dinner together."

"Well, I do need to eat," I tell him.

"So, you only want me for my food, then?"

Eyeing him across the table, I pick up my drink and take a sip. His eyes are locked on me, and I can feel his gaze deep in my soul. Staring back at him, my insides warm. There's something about this man I'm drawn to, but I just got out of a relationship with an egotistical asshole. I promised myself I'd hit the single scene for a while, but then again, a woman has needs. As much as my vibrator gets me off each and every time, nothing beats riding a real dick. Maybe I can let loose for one night, but on my terms. I mean, what harm could one night with a sexy-as-hell man be? "Very well then, Bastian, I'll have dinner with you, but I have one condition."

"And what might that be?" He picks up his glass and I watch him take a sip, and swallow. The bob of his Adam's apple is mesmerizing as the amber liquid slides down his throat.

Leaning across the table, I beckon him to me and whisper, "I want your cock for dessert."

He chokes at my statement, and I kind of feel bad for him, but he quickly recovers. "Well, since we're in the negotiating phase, after your dessert, I want your pussy for a nightcap."

"Deal," I agree.

Outstretching my hand to seal the deal with a handshake, he places his palm in mine, and an electrical current zaps from him to me. Every nerve ending in my body comes alive, and suddenly, I'm no longer hungry for dinner, I want to head straight to dessert.

After finishing our drinks, Bastian makes a call, and when we step outside, there's a car waiting at the curb for us. *Who is this man?* I think to myself as I climb into the waiting vehicle after smiling at the driver. He opens the door for me, and I lower myself into the car, sliding across the buttery-soft leather seat. Bastian and the driver chat, but I can't catch what they're saying. Bastian claps the driver on the back and climbs in next to me. Once the driver is seated, he puts his turn signal on and pulls out into traffic.

After about ten minutes, we pull up outside one of Chicago's most famous steakhouses, Courtney's Steakhouse. My stomach rumbles, and I realize I haven't eaten since breakfast. Suddenly, I'm starving. A smile graces my face as I think about all the yummy food. Such a stark contrast to what I was thinking back at the bar, but I tell myself I need sustenance if I'm going to have a night of wild sex with a relative stranger. A stranger who has me intrigued. He's clearly rich, but he doesn't come across as a pompous, rich asshole.

Bastian climbs out and offers me his hand. Like back at Bin 501, when our palms touch, a current zaps through me. I've never had such a visceral reaction to a man like this before. I should be scared, but I'm not. I'm excited to see where the night is going to go. I've told myself I only have one night with the man, so I may as well enjoy every second of it. Come morning, I'll go on my merry way with a full stomach and memories that will hopefully stay with me for a long time to come.

"Your table is ready," the hostess says as we enter.

"Thank you." Bastian nods and smiles at her. The hostess's cheeks turn pink, and she smiles seductively at him. That little lip lift has me wanting to claw her eyes out. The thought baffles me, because this is nothing but dinner and, hopefully, amazing sex.

Dropping his hand to my lower back, he ushers me farther into the restaurant. Walking past seated diners, we head deeper into the room and up a few stairs to a private table hidden behind a planter box, giving us privacy from the rest of the patrons.

Ever the gentleman, he pulls my chair out for me, and I sit down. He takes the seat across from me. "Can I get you any drinks to start?" the hostess asks.

Bastian looks at me. "What would you like to drink?"

"Martini, dirty."

"And for you, sir?"

"Whiskey, neat," he tells her, but his gaze is locked on me. With our drink order taken, she walks away, leaving us alone.

"Come here often?" I ask, breaking the silence between us.

"Considering I own half of this place, yes, I do."

"You own this place?"

"Well, I own half of it in a silent manner."

"How did that come about?" He doesn't seem like a restaurant owner, and I'm genuinely intrigued, but then again, what does the owner of a restaurant look like? "Tristian and I went to business school together, and after we graduated, we went our separate ways. A few years later, he and his partner, Courtney, moved to Chicago and we reconnected. Court's a phenomenal chef and has worked all around the world. She'd always dreamed of owning her own steakhouse." He chuckles to himself. I raise my eyebrows at him. "Courtney is from Texas, and it seems you can take the girl out of Texas, but you can't take Texas out of the girl. This place had been on the market for a while, but it was out of his price range. He and I were having drinks one night, and he was telling me all about it, so I suggested I come on board as a silent partner. I provided half the capital, and five years later, Courtney's Steakhouse is thriving. It has two Michelin stars, and anyone who is famous has dined here. Most nights are a full house, and that's because there's no better place to get a steak."

"That's amazing," I tell him, and I mean it. I don't know what he does for a living, but I can tell he cares about his friends, and that's admirable. The world can be a lonely place at times, and without the support of my friend group, I would be lonely. I bounced from foster home to foster home when I was a child. Both of my parents were killed in a freak boating accident when I was five. With no other living relatives, I became a ward of the state until I was thirteen, and I found my forever home. Karen and Terry McKeown adopted me, and I officially became a McKeown. They officially adopted me when I was seventeen, and I happily took their last name because I was finally home. I went from being orphaned Audrey Dean to Audrey McKeown, daughter and big sister. But when I was nineteen, fate struck again, and I lost my family when a drunk driver ran them down. I was delayed at work, and had I been with them, I no doubt would have lost my life as well. If it hadn't been for my friends from college, Nicole and Rebecca, I would have fallen apart. Those two girls rallied around me and got me through the second toughest thing to ever happen to me.

Our waitress returns, and I'm snapped back to the present. She places our drinks before us and smiles at Bastian like the hostess did, leaving me snarling at her internally. Can she not see he's here with me? "Courtney is preparing your meals, and the appetizer won't be too long."

Looking quizzically at him, I furrow my brows.

"Court never lets me choose when I dine here. She cooks what she feels I will like, and sometimes she uses me as a guinea pig for new dishes."

"What if you don't like what she serves?"

"That's never happened."

Over the next few hours, Bastian and I eat, laugh, and drink. After our drinks on arrival, he ordered a bottle of red, and we're onto our second bottle now. The food has been amazing, just like I knew it would be.

Placing my cutlery onto my empty plate, I grab the napkin and wipe my mouth. "Oh my God, that was the best steak I've ever had!" And I mean that. It was so tender that you could probably cut it with a butter knife. The vegetables were cooked to perfection, and the sauce? Chef's kiss. "Steak has been ruined for me now."

"That's what I like to hear." Looking up, I see a tall, slender woman standing beside our table. Her dark locks are in a messy bun on top of her head, and she's wearing a chef's uniform, leading me to surmise this is the famous Courtney.

"Court," Bastian says as he stands up and pulls her in for a hug. He kisses her on the cheek, and I internally growl at the contact. My jealousy, again, shocks me, because Bastian isn't mine, we are nothing to one another. "How are you?"

"Ready to fall into bed. Today has been crazy, but I wouldn't have it any other way." She turns her attention my way. She assesses me before speaking. "I hope Bastian is behaving."

"So far, yes," I tell her. "And thank you for dinner. That was the best steak I've ever had."

"Thank you, I appreciate your kind words." Her cheeks darken at the compliment, and I love that she's not one of those cocky, pretentious chefs. "Just wanted to stop by before I head out. You should try the chocolate mousse infused with Kahlua and cream—it's divine. Not too sweet, and not too bitter."

"I think Audrey had other ideas for dessert." He winks at me and Courtney smacks him in the arm. Meanwhile, my mouth drops open in shock.

"Good luck with him," Courtney says to me. She turns to Bastian. "And, you. Behave."

Without another word, she leaves Bastian and me alone. He drops back into his seat and stares across the table at me. The temperature around us seems to suddenly rise. "So, Audrey. What will you be having for dessert?"

5

BASTIAN

"So, Audrey, what will you be having for dessert?" I ask her, hoping she wants what I want for dessert—her mouth around my dick.

"Well, I did want your cock, but chocolate mousse infused with Kahlua and cream sure does sound delicious, if you ask me."

"Really?" I can't believe she wants dessert, real dessert, but as I sit here and stare at her, I suddenly get the image of licking chocolate mousse off of her naked body.

She starts to laugh, confusing me. "I'm just joking. I couldn't fit another thing in—"

"I'm sure I can fit," I interrupt her.

She shakes her head, but I notice her cheeks have darkened, and her nipples have turned into stiff peaks under her dress. "You, sir, are incorrigible. I still want you for dessert so what do you say, shall we get out of here?"

"Check please," I playfully call out, causing Audrey to laugh once again. She throws her head back, arching her neck. I stare at the woman who has put me under her spell. She's a knockout to look at, and don't get me started on her curves. Fuck me.

Suddenly, I have the urge to lean over and lick up the column of her neck before I swipe everything off this table and have her for dessert, right here in the middle of the restaurant. I want to grip onto her hips and slam into her over and over. But then there's her mind, she speaks freely and knows what she wants. I don't know much about her, but I want to know more. That thought alone should scare me, I've never wanted to do the whole girlfriend thing, but I could quite easily see myself dating, and falling for, this elusive woman.

"You are something else, Bastian, and I'm glad you found me again."

"I will always find you, Audrey. Now, what do you say we get out of here?"

She nods and bites her bottom lip.

Pulling my wallet out, I throw a couple of bills down on the table, knowing full well that Court is going to blow my phone up tomorrow, telling me I didn't need to pay. She calls it "perks of being a partner" but I call it "tipping the staff to continue doing an amazing job." It's purely selfish on my account because happy staff means happy diners. And happy diners mean good reviews, and good reviews mean the place is packed, and a full house is great for the bank balance.

Standing up, I walk around to her side of the table and help her up, with our hands clasped, we exit the restaurant and climb into the waiting car. As soon as the door closes, I lean forward and press the button to close the divider, earning myself a shit-eating grin from Hector through the rearview mirror.

Turning in my seat to face Audrey, I find her staring at me. She bites her bottom lip, her teeth digging into the skin. Reaching out, I pull her lip free. The urge to lean across and sink my teeth into her lip, marking and claiming her, is strong, but the minx she is, beats me to it. She nips at my thumb, gently biting the tip. Pulling my finger free, I bring it to my lips and lick over the indents she left behind. Shaking my head, I reach out again and cup her cheek in my palm. Running the pad of my thumb over her jawline, she shudders under my touch and the already heated air in the car heats further.

Audrey leans into my hand, and with her eyes steadfastly locked on mine, she rubs her face against my palm. Sliding my hand around the back of her neck, I thread my fingers into her hair and gently tug on the strands, earning myself a moan. That sound travels straight to my dick, and it twitches, threatening to bust through my zipper.

Closing the distance between us, I lean across the seat and tug her toward me, slamming my lips to hers in a bruising kiss. Holding her cheeks in my hands, I push my tongue in her mouth. I've wanted to do this since I saw her sitting in Bin 501 three days ago. I may have started the kiss, but Audrey takes control when she shimmies closer and climbs into my lap, deepening the kiss and our connection.

Straddling me, she holds on to my face and continues to kiss me.

This is the best fucking kiss of my life. It's slow yet sensual. Hungry yet soft. Her tongue dances with mine, and when she begins to grind herself on me, I'm ready to blow like a fucking teenager when, thankfully, Hector's voice comes through, advising us we have arrived.

"To be continued," I murmur against Audrey's lips.

She nods and reluctantly climbs off me. Her eyes drop to my crotch, and they widen when she sees my cock straining against the material of my pants. "Looks like you have a bit of a problem."

Shaking my head, I stare into her emerald-green eyes. "I'm fine, but as soon as we get upstairs, it's game on. And Audrey, I play to win."

"I play to win too, so you better bring your A game."

Fuck me, I think I've met my match in this woman, and I cannot wait to see what happens next.

Opening the door, I climb out and offer her my hand. She takes it, and I help her out. "Have a good night, sir," Hector says from the front of the car.

"Ohh, I plan to. See you in the morning, Hector."

He nods and I close the car door. Taking her hand in mine, I tug her across the pavement and into the building. The doorman nods and opens the door for us. We quickly make our way across the lobby and into the waiting elevator. Pressing the button for the penthouse, the doors close, and when we're locked in, I pounce.

Pushing her up against the wall of the elevator, I grind my crotch into her and cover her mouth with mine. Sliding my hand down her side, I squeeze her thigh, and without any further prompting, she lifts her leg and wraps it around my ass, pulling me closer to her. She rubs herself against my growing erection, and if I thought I was hard in the car before, now I'm harder than steel.

The elevator doors behind us open, and not wanting to let her go, I lift her up into my arms. She wraps her other leg around my waist, and I exit the elevator.

My lips are locked to hers, and my body is thrumming with desire, want, and need for her. I need to get her naked and sink myself deep inside of her.

Right now, I'm thankful to have a thumb scanner in place of a key. Pressing my thumb to the screen, the door lock disengages, and I push it open. Kicking it closed with my foot, I take her bag from her shoulder and drop it onto the entrance table.

Striding across the room, I head down the hallway toward my bedroom. Leaving the lights off, I stalk over to the bed and place Audrey down on her feet. Breathlessly, we both stand here, our chests puffing. "You need to get naked so I can have my dessert."

"I thought I was having you for dessert?" she sasses back.

"You can have yours later, because right now, I need to fuck you. I need to feel your pussy clench around my dick. I need to feel you come apart beneath me as I fuck you like you've never been fucked before."

"I think I'd like that, so I will happily forgo my dessert."

"Excellent, now strip."

"So bossy."

"You haven't seen bossy yet," I warn her. "Now remove your clothes, or I will tear them off of you and you will be leaving here tomorrow in nothing."

Reaching behind her, she lowers the zipper of her dress. Pulling one strap down, I'm given a view of her lace-covered tit. She slides the other one down, and the material falls to her waist. Wriggling her hips, her dress flutters to the carpet, giving me an unobstructed view of her lingerie-clad body.

"You are exquisite, Audrey."

"Why thank you, but we seem to have a problem."

"And what's that?"

"You have too many clothes on."

"Yes, I do, but I believe I told *you* to get naked."

"Ohh, I will, but fair's fair when it comes to getting naked."

"If it means I get to see you in nothing but those sexy-as-fuck heels, then sure, I'll get naked with you."

Untucking my shirt, I kick off my shoes, while I make quick work of the buttons and slide the material down my arms, where it joins her dress on the carpet. With my eyes locked on hers, I flick open the button on my slacks, lower the fly, and push my pants down, kicking them to the side.

"Commando?" she asks. "That's very forward of you."

"Look closer," I tell her. She drops her gaze and smiles when she sees my briefs inside. Lifting her gaze back to my dick, her eyes widen when she gets a closer look. "Afraid?" I taunt. She shakes her head and intently watches as I grip my shaft and begin to stroke. "Now it seems that *you* are the overdressed one."

Without uttering a word, she removes her remaining clothing, and I can't decide if seeing her naked or in lingerie is sexier, but the winner becomes clear when she climbs onto my bed, crawls up the mattress, and lies down. She lies there on the bed, naked as the day she was born, except for her heels, and never have I seen a more stunning female.

Her tits are plump, she has a slight roll to her stomach, but she doesn't let it bother her. Her legs go on and on, and her pussy, fuck me, it's glistening. Weeping for my cock.

"I'm going to fuck you hard and fast, Drey, and then I'm going to fuck you nice and slow. And tomorrow, every time you move, you will feel me. Think of me. Want me again."

"I think you're all talk, Bastian."

"You think so?" She nods and bites her lower lip, and like in the car only moments ago, I want to bite and devour it ... and her.

Something passes behind her eyes, and with a sexy-as-fuck smirk and her gaze locked on mine, she snakes her hand down her abdomen and between her thighs. Before me, she spreads her legs and begins to circle her finger over her clit before she slips her digit inside.

Watching her pleasure herself is erotic as hell. My dick weeps at the scene before me. She thinks she's in control, but two can play at that game and little does she know, I always win.

Standing at the end of my bed, I stroke my cock in time to her finger sliding in and out of her dripping slit. Her eyes droop closed, and her body stiffens. She lets out a sound that has my cock twitching. Her head tilts back, once again elongating her neck, and she gives herself over to the pleasure of her orgasm. Watching her come apart from her fingers is highly erotic, and I cannot wait to see her come apart on my dick.

Her eyes open, and she smiles when she sees me staring at her. She brings her hand to her lips and licks her release from her fingers. "Hmmmpf, seems I got my dessert after all."

"Ohh, baby." I rest my knee on the edge of the bed and lower myself down. I crawl up her body, and once she's trapped beneath me, I gaze down at her. "Dessert hasn't even started."

6

———

AUDREY

SWALLOWING DEEPLY, it hits me: I may have met my match. This man is intriguing on so many levels, and I cannot wait to see what happens next. Leaning down, he presses his lips to mine, his tongue licking in my mouth. He groans, he can taste me on my lips. And not to toot my own horn, but I taste divine.

His tongue plunges in and out of my mouth, and the longer we kiss, the more my desire increases. Swiveling my hips beneath him, I can feel his cock against my thigh, but that's not where I want it.

He pulls back, and I mourn his loss, but when I realize he's reaching into his side table drawer, I'm okay with it. I'm glad he's thinking straight, because I would have fucked him bare. Yes, I'm on the pill, but that pill won't protect me from an STD, and I don't know this man's medical history. I know I'm clean. I've never not used protection before, and I'm not about to start now.

Pushing himself upright, he tears open the foil packet with his teeth. Pulling out the condom, he tosses the wrapper to the side, and I watch as he sheathes this cock. Once it's on, he strokes himself a few times before he lines his cock up with my slit. With a flick of his hips, he sinks himself inside of me. The feeling of him sliding inside me is indescribable, and I throw my head back in ecstasy. Closing my eyes, I give myself over to the pleasure and him.

Leaning down, he covers my body with his before licking up my neck. His tongue leaves a wet trail along my skin, and I want him to lick me again and again. I want him to lick me everywhere, it's as if his tongue is liquid cocaine and I'm addicted to the high.

He peppers kisses on my exposed neck as he thrusts in and out of me, but it's not enough, I need more. "Kiss me," I command.

And kiss me he does.

His tongue plunges into my mouth and begins an erotic dance. Slipping. Sliding. Caressing. The heady combination of his tongue in my mouth and his cock inside of me is fantastic. This man has ruined kisses and sex for me, no one will ever compare. It almost makes me want more than just one night, but right now, one night is all I can offer.

Shaking off that thought, I focus on the here and now. I don't want to miss a minute of this. I'm glad I started to focus, because Bastian flips me over onto my stomach, lifts my hips, slaps my ass, and drives back into me. His balls slapping against my thighs as his dick hits *the* spot deep within.

It's pleasure overload but at the same time, it's not enough. Sliding my hand beneath me, I press on my clit and that feeling that leads to a massive explosion begins to simmer.

Bastian's fingers dig into my hips, no doubt it will bruise, and I'm here for it.

This is carnal.

It's animalistic.

It's fucking amazing. I'm soaring higher and higher toward my release. He slides his arm around my middle and pulls me upright. My back to his front and his dick, his magical dick, continues to slam into me.

Holding me to him, he cups my breasts in his palms and, once again, licks and kisses my neck. I've never had someone lick me before, and I can't believe I've been missing out. "Yes," I hiss when he gently tugs on my nipple.

Leaning my head back onto his shoulder, I gaze up at him. He really is gorgeous. Reaching my arm behind his head, I guide him down to my lips. Kissing him like this is awkward, but kissing this man is fast becoming a favorite hobby of mine.

With our lips locked, he plays with my boobs as he thrusts in and out of me. Each movement hitting deeper and deeper, bringing me closer to release.

"Come for me," he demands.

It's on my lips to tell him to fuck off. No one bosses

me around. He slides one of his hands down my stomach and plays with my clit. He alternates between pressing on the tight bundle of nerves and gently tugging on it. He twists my nipple and clit at the same time, and it's game over.

Dropping my head, a feral sound passes through my lips as it hits. My back arches. My body tightens. Every inch of my skin tingles as the most intense, most euphoric orgasm snakes through my body.

From head to toe, I feel my release. Throwing my head back, I scream as the last of my release cascades over me. My undoing sets him off. He holds me tight to him as he empties himself into the condom. Grunting in that sexy manly way when he comes.

Both of us are breathing heavily as we come back to Earth.

I'm still cocooned in his embrace, and with the grace of an angel, he lowers us both to the mattress and spoons me from behind.

I'm not usually one for cuddling after sex, but this is nice, and that niceness increases when he places a swift kiss on my neck. Smiling, I give myself over to the moment, which has left me feeling all warm and fuzzy. I think I found my new addiction, move over forehead kisses, neck kisses are my new favorite type of kiss.

Lying here, I happily drift off to sleep in Bastian's arms, well fucked and completely sated.

Waking a few hours later, we're still in the same position. My bladder is full, and I need to empty it before I wet the bed. Wriggling around, I untangle myself from Bastian's embrace and make my way into the en suite. Closing the door, I flick on the light and my eyes widen at the room. It's the most exquisite bathroom I've ever seen. There's a double vanity, a separate shower, and a free-standing tub with incredible views of the Chicago River. There are floor-to-ceiling windows. White marble tiles and a stunning charcoal feature wall.

Using the facilities, I flush, and while I wash my hands, I gaze at my reflection. I notice a love bite on my neck and shake my head. Drying my hands, I lift my arm and run my fingertip over the purple mark. I mumble, "Asshole," as I pad over to the window.

Staring out at the city I love, I shiver, but the coolness is replaced when a warm body wraps their arms around me from behind. Closing my eyes, I lean my head back on his shoulder, and he gently kisses my neck. Spinning around in his arms, I drape mine over his shoulders and kiss him. His tongue caresses mine. His cock thickens, pressing into my stomach. Sliding one hand between us, I grab his shaft in my palm and gently stroke. Breaking the kiss, I drop to my knees and skate my tongue over his tip. Earning a hiss from him, I open wide and suck. He threads his fingers into my hair and guides me up and down his shaft. He tugs on the strands, and it only heightens my want for this man. I'm glad he found me again, because this has been the best night of my life. Focusing on the task at hand, I increase the pressure as I hollow my cheeks and relax my throat. Taking him all the way in, his pubic hairs tickle my nose but that's the least of my worries. When I cup his balls and press on his perineum, his body stiffens, and with his dick wedged in my throat, he comes. Spurt after spurt fills my throat, almost choking me. Sensing my fear, he pulls back a little and lets me lick him clean.

Resting back on my haunches, we silently stare at one another as I wipe at the corner of my mouth, licking the pad of my finger in what I hope is a seductive manner.

"Well, that was unexpected," he says, breaking the silence in the bathroom.

"A good unexpected, I hope."

"Very good, indeed. I take it you enjoyed your dessert?"

"Was definitely worth the wait."

"Happy to oblige, but now, it's my turn for my nightcap."

7

———

BASTIAN

SWOOPING her up into my arms, I walk back into the bedroom and gently lower her down to the mattress. She lifts herself up onto her elbows and watches as I lower to my knees.

"Open," I command, and like a good girl, she spreads her legs for me, and I finally get a look at her. The first time around, I was too eager to please and I didn't get a chance to admire her and, fuck me, like she just said, it is worth the wait.

Her slit is glistening, waiting for me to lick and devour it. "Did sucking my cock turn you on, Audrey?" She nods and bites her lip.

"It took all my effort not to finger myself."

"Well, have at it," I tell her, sitting back on my heels, I wait for her to do as I asked.

"You want me to have your nightcap?"

"No." I shake my head. "I want you to get started. I

want you to finger yourself just like you wanted to while my dick was in your mouth and down your throat. I want you to draw forth your orgasm. I want you to be a quivering mess, but you will not come. You hear me, Audrey? You will not come, because it will be *me* finishing what you started. Your orgasm is mine."

"As you wish," she agrees, and ever so slowly, she slides her hand between her thighs. There is nothing more erotic than watching a woman pleasure herself. Who knows what buttons to push better than the recipient? It's also purely selfish, because it allows me to watch so I can become a master, THE master, at feasting on her pussy. I can watch, learn, and improve on what she does.

Sliding her finger into her slit, her lips part, and she moans in the sexiest way. My eyes are locked between her thighs, and I steadfastly watch her finger disappear inside of her, only to return slick with her arousal.

My dick throbs at the sight before me. I cannot wait to sink back into her. Her pussy was made for me. After just one taste, I know I'm going to be addicted. One night with the woman is not going to be enough. A millennium with her would never be enough. Audrey "whatever her last name is" is the forbidden fruit. The ultimate prize and I'm never letting her go.

Her finger continues to slide in and out of her pussy, while her other hand massages her breasts, tugging on her nipples. Her delectable pink nipples.

I don't know where to look. It's sensory overload.

Her back arches, and I know she's close, but she can't come yet. Her release is mine, and when she comes, it's going to be all over my tongue.

Moving between her legs, I push her hand out of the way and lower my face to her slit. Licking from taint to clit, I almost come on the spot when her sweet, sweet nectar hits my tongue. "You taste exquisite," I murmur as I continue to lap at her slit.

Gripping her hips in my palms, I hold her tightly as I lick, suck, and inhale her juices and scent like a starved man. Circling her clit with my tongue, she writhes beneath me and moans loudly, the sound heading straight to my dick. I can't decide if I want to fuck her or continue to dine on her.

"Yesssssss," she mewls, adding extra s's to the word. The decision is taken away from me when she slides her hands into my hair and shoves my face in deeper. She's suffocating me with her cunt, and if I die right now, I'd die a happy fucking man.

Lifting my gaze, I stare up at her. Her eyes are closed, and her face has a euphoric look on it. Her body glistens with a light sheen of sweat, her skin is a flushed shade of pink. Her nipples are tight and taut. Never have I seen anything, or anyone, more perfect. Her legs squeeze my head tighter, and I can tell she's close.

I'm ready to watch her shatter before I fuck her into a coma. Removing one hand from her hip, I slide a finger into her while I focus on her clit with my lips and tongue.

"Fuck. Yes," she hisses. "Yes. Yes, fucking, yes."

Inserting another finger, her walls tighten around my digits, and I feel her body stiffen. I bite down on her clit, and she screams as her orgasm unleashes. My fingers pump, and I suck on her nub as she gives herself over to the pleasure.

Her body relaxes into the mattress beneath her, and before she can open her eyes, I spread her legs wide, and with a flick of my hips, I thrust deep inside her.

Green eyes stare up at me as my hips piston back and forth. Lifting her legs, she wraps them around me, holding me tight to her. With my eyes locked on hers, I fuck her hard and fast. Her pussy was made for my dick, and before I know it, we're both crashing over the edge, moaning each other's name. Grunting and groaning, I empty myself inside of her.

Collapsing onto the mattress beside her, we both lie here, panting. Turning our heads, we stare at one another. Reaching up, I cup her cheek in my palm. Leaning toward her, I press my lips to hers. With our lips locked, we roll onto our sides and stare at one another before we blissfully drift off to sleep.

Sunlight filters into the room the next morning, and when I open my eyes, I see the spot next to me is vacant, again. Climbing out of bed, I walk into the en suite but it's empty. Exiting the room, I head out to the kitchen, hoping to find her at the coffee machine, but when I enter the living area, I'm still alone.

Spinning around, I look at the entrance table and notice her bag is missing. "What the fuck?" I growl as it hits me—she's gone.

She snuck out.

Shaking my head, I run my hands through my hair. Sneaking out is my thing. This is the first time a woman has ever fucked and ducked on me, and I have to say, I don't like it.

Walking back into my bedroom, I stare at the crumpled sheets on my bed and memories of last night come back to me in all their Technicolor glory. Last night with Audrey was amazing, and I want more. I found her once before, and I will find her again, if it's the last thing I do.

8

AUDREY

...two months later

"ATTENTION, all passengers, this is an announcement regarding Flight 152. We regret to inform you that there has been a delay in the departure of your flight. The delay is due to an engine issue. We are currently working to resolve the issue as quickly as possible. We apologize for any inconvenience this may cause. We ask that all passengers remain in the terminal and await further updates. Our team is working to provide you with the most up-to-date information regarding your flight. We appreciate your patience and understanding during this time. Thank you for choosing..."

"For fuck's sake," I hiss.

Shaking my head, I sit back in my seat and stare out the terminal window. Rain pours down from the sky above, and I watch a group of workers in bright yellow jackets down below. They're standing in a huddle, staring up at the plane. A flap on the engine is open and there's a guy up on a ladder with his head inside. From where I'm sitting, it appears that very little work is being done, but then again, I know nothing about aircrafts.

A bright fork of lightning lights up the night sky and seconds later, a crack of thunder loudly claps. This trip was a disaster from the beginning, and the angry sky outside just adds to my foul mood. My flight here yesterday was diverted due to a storm. Then I slept through my alarm this morning, and I only just made the interview but as soon as I walked in, I knew something was wrong.

My Spidey senses were on high alert, and I walked out of there dejected. I knew the job was too good to be true, and we all know what they say about that. Plus, I didn't trust my gut, and now I'm delayed in New York.

Don't get me wrong, New York is no place to sneeze at, but I just want my bed. Grabbing my bag, I walk to the closest bar, and finally, luck is on my side. There's a vacant seat at the bar. Dropping down into it, I smile at the bartender.

"What can I get you?"

"Martini, dirty," I tell the man.

With a nod, he turns around and goes about making my drink. A few moments later, he places my drink in front of me. Handing over my card, I pay for my drink and then lift the glass to my lips and take a sip. Closing my eyes, I smile to myself at the deliciousness in my mouth, but my eyes fly open when next to me a deep voice utters, "Whiskey, neat."

I'd recognize that voice anywhere, and when I turn my head, I come face-to-face with Bastian. He smiles down at me from his standing position, and my breath hitches because it really is him.

"Audrey," he drawls out my name, and my body shivers as I remember him hissing my name as he came inside me.

"Bastian," I stammer, "w-w-w-what are you doing here?" As I wait for him to answer me, my heart rate kicks up and my panties, well, they're soaked just from looking at him ... and hearing him say my name. *I'm such a ho! Who gets turned on just by someone saying their name?* It's me. I'm the ho.

For the past two months, this man has starred in my dreams, and it's been his face I imagine as I pleasure myself at home. After one night, he's ruined me for all other men. Not that there's been another man since him, I'm not *that* sort of ho. I'm the sort of ho who imagines her one-night stand during self-gratification moments and whose panties dampen when he says her name.

"Fancy meeting you here," he says, ignoring my question, but really, what else would he be doing in an airport? Like me, he's clearly waiting for a flight home. *What was he doing in New York?* "What brings you to New York?" The sound of his voice snaps me back to the present. Sitting here, I watch him pick up the tumbler and take a sip. His blue eyes never leave mine as he drinks. He implores me with his eyes to answer.

"Business," I reply. A silence envelops us, and at the same time, everything and everyone around us fades into the background. "What are you doing here?" I ask when the silence becomes too much.

"Waiting for a flight. You?"

"Same," I tell him.

"Flight 152?"

"Yep." I nod. "You?"

He repeats my answer and pulls out the chair next to me, taking a seat. Silently, we stare at one another, sipping on our drinks. He really is handsome, even more so than I remember. The scruff on his face is a little longer than when I saw him last, and now, I'm imagining what it will be like to feel it between my thighs.

He opens his mouth just as an announcement starts, "Thank you for your patience, ladies and gentlemen..." Before she even continues, I know what she's about to say. "Unfortunately"—called it—"I don't have good news. Flight 152 has been canceled, and all other flights have been grounded due to weather. Please proceed to the nearest service counter, and you will be put on alternate flights. We apologize for the inconvenience, but your safety is our priority. Thank you for your cooperation regarding this weather delay."

A chorus of angry cries fills the air, but there's no

point in getting angry, the airline staff can't control the weather. In the grand scheme of things, this is just the cherry on the top of this trip's shittastic cake. Waving down the bartender, I order another martini.

He quickly places my drink down, and I chug it back like a frat boy at a kegger.

"Rough day?" Bastian asks.

"You could say that."

"Mine was shit but it's suddenly looking up."

"How are all flights being grounded looking up?" I air quote, looking up, because from where I'm sitting, things are *not* looking up.

"I ran into you, and now, it looks like we're stranded, which means"—he leans into me—"I get to have another nightcap with you."

"Is that so?"

He nods and grins. "Would you like to have a nightcap with me?"

Waving the bartender over, I keep my gaze on Bastian's and say, "Check, please."

9

BASTIAN

I couldn't believe my luck when I saw Audrey stand up after the delay announcement. She grabbed her carry-on case and turned toward the bar I was sitting in. From my position, I watched her stride across the terminal toward me, well, the bar. Her heels clicked on the floor, and like a lion stalking his prey, I watched her. Her black skirt hugged her ass, and the pink blouse she was wearing was understated but highlights her curves and tits. Of all the airports and bars in the world, she and I just so happen to be in the same one. What are the chances?

When all flights are cancelled, I take it as a sign from above that this woman and I are meant to have another night together. While I wait for her answer, I realize I'm going to be devastated if she turns me down. After what feels like an eternity, she utters two magical words, *check please.* Offering up a silent prayer to Mother Nature, I wait for her to join me.

At first, I was pissed off due to the delay, but now, not so much.

She settles her bill, refusing to let me pay, and then the two of us exit the terminal. It's busy outside, full of disgruntled travelers, but somehow, I manage to hail a taxi without too much fuss. "The Luxe Hotel in Manhattan, please," I tell the driver.

"That's a bit fancy," she states, as the driver pulls away from the curb.

"It's the only place to stay when in New York ... or Hawaii." Hunter Crawford and I crossed paths a few years ago, and we became fast friends. He now lives in Hawaii with his wife and son. That was a drama and a half and would make one hell of a romance novel. You see, he and Sully had a one-night stand, and then years later, their paths crossed again. She was now a single mom ... with his kid. Turns out, he knocked her up, but since they only exchanged nicknames during the night they spent together, it's kinda hard to track someone down via only a nickname. Fate, however, seemed to have a plan for them, because now, they're happily married and expecting again.

The storm has caused mayhem on the roads, and it takes nearly two hours to get from the airport to the hotel. While stuck, I call ahead and book us a room. The taxi pulls into the valet area, I pay the fare, and we climb out. Taking her hand in mine, we head inside.

Crossing the lobby, we make our way over to reception and I check us in.

With the room key in hand, we walk to the elevators and wait. The doors open, and we step in. Leaning over, I press the button for our floor. Both of us stare ahead as the metal car whisks us up forty floors, and with a ding, the doors open, and we step out.

Placing my hand on her lower back, I escort her to our suite. Swiping the card over the reader, the light flashes green and a loud beep echoes in the otherwise silent hallway. Pushing down on the handle, I push on the door and step aside.

"Thanks," Audrey murmurs as she glides past me, her suitcase trailing behind her. I'm assaulted with her perfume, and my cock appreciates her scent and starts to harden.

Audrey wheels her suitcase into the living area and drops her handbag onto the sofa. She walks over to the floor-to-ceiling windows and looks out into the darkness. A lightning bolt lights up the night sky, and I see her reflection in the glass. She really is gorgeous, more gorgeous than I remember.

Coming up behind her, I rest my hands on her hips, and she shudders at my touch. Leaning in, I brush her blonde locks away and pepper her neck with kisses. She tilts her head to the side, giving me better access. Nibbling her earlobe, she leans back into me, and I slide my arms around her waist, reaching up to cup her tits.

Lifting her arms up, she runs her hand up my neck and into my hair. She scrapes her fingernails over my scalp and gently pulls on my hair.

Spinning her around, I cover her mouth with mine. Her tongue pushes past my lips, and I suck. She presses her chest into mine, plastering herself to me. Backing her into the window, I continue to fuck her mouth with my tongue.

Breaking the kiss, I whisper, "I do believe you owe me a nightcap." Before she can reply, I drop to my knees, slide my hands up her legs and under her skirt. Pushing up the material until it's bunched around her waist, I grin when I see a wet spot on her panties. Before I think about what I'm doing, I lean forward and suck.

"O," she pants, and her 'o' turns into an "oooooo" when I push the material to the side and lick her from taint to clit. Pressing my face into her, I devour her cunt with my mouth and tongue.

Inserting a finger, her walls clench around me, and her juices coat my hand. The sounds coming from her are carnal and have my dick close to bursting through my fly. Her nectar smears across my tongue and chin. There's so much liquid pouring out of her that I could drown ... and I'd die a happy man.

She clutches the strands of my hair in her fingers and tugs when her orgasm crashes into her. She rides my face, suffocating and drowning me. Just when I feel like I'm going to pass out, her body relaxes, and I inhale deeply. Sucking in a lungful of air, I pull back and gaze up at her, both of us panting.

"That was…"

"Mmmhmpf," I reply as I push myself up into a standing position. Caging her against the glass, I stare into her eyes. "What are you doing to me?"

"What are you doing to me?" she throws back with a wink. Reaching for me, she adds, "I need to fuck you now."

Audrey is literally me but in woman form. I've met my match, and I know that, like last time, I'm going to want more.

10

AUDREY

"I need you to fuck me now," I tell him, as I reach for his pants to grip his cock.

"Fuuuuuck," he hisses, and I inwardly high-five myself. Men think they're so tough but wrap your hand or mouth around their dicks, and they become putty in your hand—or mouth.

"I can't decide if I want you to wrap your lips around my dick or if I want to sink myself balls deep inside of you."

"Why not both?" I offer.

"I like the way you think, Drey. Now, lie back and let me feast on your taco."

"Did you just refer to my vagina as a taco?"

"I sure did—"

"Bastian," I scold, "don't ruin tacos for me."

He chuckles. "You love my dirty mouth."

"Yes, yes, I do, and since you're taking your time

and thinking about tacos, I'm taking over. Right now, I want your dick in my mouth. Then, I want you to fuck me against this window for all of New York to see. Then, you're going to feed me tacos, and then you're going to fuck me into a coma."

"Where have you been all my life?"

Shrugging, I drop to my knees and stare up at him. "The time for talking is over, Bastian. It's time to get down and dirty."

"Have at it, gorgeous."

And have at it I do.

Pulling out his dick, I lick over the tip. Twirling my tongue around the head, I lick down his shaft to his balls. Sucking one into my mouth, it pops out. I repeat the action to his other one before I trail my tongue back up to the tip. Opening my mouth, I lower my head down and swallow his shaft until his tip hits my tonsils. Loosening my throat, I suck him down until my nose presses against his stomach.

My head bobs back and forth, his shaft sliding in and out of my mouth and throat.

"Fuck, Audrey," he growls from above. "Your mouth is heaven."

Smirking with my mouth full, I double down, sucking and licking harder. My hand alternates between pumping his dick and playing with his balls.

Sliding his fingers into my hair, he takes over and guides my head. Taking care not to be too rough, but at the same time, giving himself over to the pleasure my mouth is laving upon him.

"I'm ... I'm..." he stammers, and before he can finish his sentence, the first spray of hot, salty cum hits the back of my throat. Swallowing every last drop, his dick pops free and I stare up at him from my position on the floor. "That was phenomenal, Audrey."

"Thank you," I murmur, hearing him praising my blow job capabilities is not something I realized I wanted, but knowing he enjoyed that has me beaming. "So, what's next?"

"I want you to stand up and strip. Then, I want you to lean back against the glass, I want you to play with your pussy, and once you're dripping, I'm going to fuck you for all of New York to see, just like you wanted."

Standing up, with my eyes locked on his, I untuck my blouse. One by one, I pop open the buttons. Leaving my shirt, I grip the zipper on my skirt and lower it. Wriggling my hips, it falls to the carpet below, and I step out of it, kicking it to the side. Finally, I remove my blouse, and it joins my skirt. Standing before him in my heels and underwear, he swallows deeply. "Like what you see?"

"Very much so," he confirms with a nod. "But I'd like to see you in only your heels."

"That can be arranged."

Reaching behind my back, I unclasp my bra and drop it to the growing clothing pile. Hooking my fingers into my panties, I roll them down my thighs and step out of them. Holding them up, they hang off my index finger. Bastian snatches them from my hand and brings them to his nose, inhaling deeply.

"Why is that so sexy?" I ask him.

"I don't know, but you, Audrey, are a vision. Turn around," he growls.

Doing as he asks, I rest my hands on the glass and lean forward. I thrust my ass toward him, and when I glance over my shoulder, I see he has his hand wrapped around his hard dick.

"Why don't you replace your hand with my pussy?"

"Ohhh, I will but first, I'm going to enjoy the view. I have to say, New York has never looked so sexy."

"I think I can make it sexier," I purr.

Spinning around, I rest my back against the glass and slip my hand between my thighs. Spreading my lips wide, I circle my clit. With my other hand, I massage and caress my breast. Tugging on my nipple, I roll it between my thumb and forefinger, moaning at the pleasure building low in my belly.

Bastian and I both moan, the sounds are highly erotic and add to the heated atmosphere within the room.

"I need you to fuck me now, Bastian."

"As you wish," he utters, and in the blink of an eye, he shucks his clothes off, sheathes his dick with a condom, lifts me up, and impales me on his cock.

"Fuuuuuck," I groan at the sudden intrusion, but my shock quickly morphs into unbridled pleasure as he begins to thrust in and out of me. Like a fine-tuned machine, my legs wrap around his hips, and we fall into a rhythm.

Up and down, I bounce on his cock.

His shaft sliding deeper and deeper.

It's hard to tell where I end and he begins. But wherever that may be, as long as he keeps fucking me like this, I don't really care.

"Kiss me," I demand out of nowhere.

"As you wish," he voices before leaning forward and pressing his lips to mine. His tongue pushes into my mouth and picks up a rhythm in sync with his dick down below.

Everything around me fades into the background. All I see, and feel, is Bastian and his dick. This man and I have an unbelievable connection in the bedroom. Never has sex with anyone felt so intense. So perfect. There's no faking it with this man, and the scream I let loose is far from fake. His magnificent dick hits that elusive spot most men cannot find, and I explode. My pussy clenches his shaft as the most intense, most electric orgasm in the history of orgasms ripples through me. My body spasms from head to toe, and my blood simmers as he works toward his release.

The sensations keep buzzing, and before I know it, I'm headfirst into another orgasm. My second release sets him off, and he grunts and groans as he follows me into nirvana.

"Fuck me," I pant when my body finally unclenches and stops vibrating.

"I just did," he cheekily says with a wink. "But I agree, that was something else."

"You've ruined me for other men."

"Please don't talk about other men while my dick is still inside you."

"Sorry, but it's the truth."

"Well, you've ruined me for other women. No woman will ever compare to you and your delectable cunt and scent."

"Hallmark should put that on a Valentine's Day card."

"I'll be sure to send in a recommendation. But first, we need to shower, refuel, and then I'm going to fuck you into a coma, and then I'm going to wake you up with my head between your thighs."

"If you insist," I playfully reply.

"Ohhh, I insist."

Spinning around, he stalks through the suite, into the master bedroom and into the en suite bathroom. Without putting me down, he steps into the shower that could easily fit a hockey team in it. He presses a button on the wall, and water begins to flow from the showerhead above. I squeal when the cold water hits my heated skin. Bastian, the bastard, chuckles and uses his body to protect me from the cool water, but it quickly heats, and he moves so the water rains down on both of us.

"You can put me down now," I tell him.

"I can, but I like having you in my arms."

"And I like being in your arms, but you need to remove the condom, and I need to clean up. I'm not going to let a UTI ruin the best sex of my life."

"Best sex of your life, huh?"

"Don't get all cocky. You know it was good."

"Good is not the adjective I would use to describe the sex between us, but I don't want you to get a UTI, so I will reluctantly put you down." He places me down on my feet, and I stumble when my feet hit the tiles. Stepping backward, I tilt my head, close my eyes, and let the water cascade down my body.

"Will you allow me to wash you?"

Lifting my head, I stare across at Bastian and his eyes are once again heated as they roam over my naked and wet body. "You just want to feel me up?"

"Maybe I do, but can you blame me? You naked and wet is a vision, Audrey. And the sex just now, is etched in my spank bank, and when I'm ninety, this night will play on repeat each and every time I plea-sure myself."

"You reckon you'll still be able to get it up when you're ninety?"

"I know so, but if I can't, I'll pop a little blue pill."

"I'd pay to see the day you pop a little blue pill."

"Well, stick with me and I won't need to. I just

need to look at your wet, naked body, and I'm ready to go. See?"

Dropping my gaze, I notice that, yes, he is once again hard. This man is like the Energizer Bunny when it comes to sex, but I can't say I'm too upset over that.

"You can wash me," I tell him, "but no hanky-panky. My vagina needs a rest if you're going to fuck me into a coma after we eat."

"Deal," he agrees ... and FYI, he fucks me again in the shower, twice, but I'm not complaining. I'm going to take what I can get, because come morning, we'll be going our separate ways, again.

11

BASTIAN

Leaving Audrey in the shower was hard—pun intended—but we need food. Audrey is just as sexual as I am. I've totally met my match with this woman. Seems fate has a plan for us since we ran into each other again, and I think this is the first time I've been happy to have a flight cancelled.

I've just hung up with room service when Audrey walks into the room. She has on the hotel-provided robe, and her hair is up in a towel, drying.

"Drink?" I offer.

"Water, please."

Nodding, I open the mini bar and grab out a bottle, handing it to her. "Food should be here soon."

"Thanks, I'm famished."

"I wonder why?" I tease.

"I wonder," she replies, taking a seat on the sofa. "Looks like the storm is passing." Just as she says that, the night sky lights up, and a few seconds later, a loud crash of thunder shakes the windows. "Oops, I think I spoke too soon."

I'm about to join her on the sofa when there's a knock at the door. *That was quick,* I think to myself. Opening the door, I furrow my brows as I stare at the concierge. "Courtesy of Mr. Crawford," he says, handing me a bottle of champagne.

"Thank you," I tell him with a nod.

Closing the door, I walk back into the room. "Who was that?" Audrey asks.

"Concierge dropped this off for us."

"That's sweet, but why?"

"I know the owner," I tell her with a shrug. "Would you like a glass?"

"It would be rude not to."

"Yes, yes it would."

Opening the bottle, I pour two glasses and hand one to her. "What shall we toast to?"

"To serendipity," she offers.

"I like it," I confirm. Raising my glass, I keep my eyes locked on hers as I repeat the toast. We tap glasses, and she takes a sip, moaning. "You moan like that again and I won't be held accountable for what I do."

"I told you in the shower, my vagina needs rest."

"Yeah, and how did that go?" I waggle my eyebrows, and she laughs.

"Shut up," she hisses, playfully slapping me on the

forearm. "But for the record, both times were your fault."

Staring at her, I shrug because she's right. The first time, I couldn't help myself after soaping up her body. Her nipples were begging for me to suckle on them and then one thing led to another. And the second, well, her soapy hands were all over my cock. What can I say, I'm a man.

Room service arrives, and we sit on the sofa eating bacon cheeseburgers, drinking champagne, and watching reruns of *Friends*. After eating, we snuggle together and eventually drift off to sleep.

Waking a few hours later, I smile when I see her still here. Scooping Audrey up into my arms, I walk us into the bedroom and lay her down on the mattress. Climbing in beside her, she burrows into me, and we have sleepy sex before drifting back into dreamland.

When I wake in the morning, I squint because we didn't close the blinds. The room is bright, and I reach to the mattress next to me, but I'm met with a cold sheet.

Sitting up, I look around and shake my head. "Son of a bitch," I hiss. Once again, Audrey is gone, and I didn't get her details.

12

AUDREY

...a few months later

After missing out on the job in New York, which sucked, and my night with Bastian—which was amazing—life kind of just floated by until last week. I was chatting with Nicole—who knew someone, who knew someone twice removed, that knew Blackstone was looking for a new editor. I reached out to them, and after emailing with Kerrie in HR, we set a date and time to meet. A week later, I met with Kerrie and the editorial director, Lainey, and before I knew what was happening, I was hired. You are now looking at an editor at Blackstone Publishing. It all happened so quickly. After signing all the paperwork, I was given a start date—and well, here we are. Today is the first day of my new job.

I'm so excited for this next venture. I'll still edit

for my indie clients. I made sure that was a clause in my contract, but my main employment will now be at Blackstone Publishing. Who knows, maybe in time, I can get a deal for some of my indie clients. It would be amazing to see their words in brick-and-mortar stores.

After getting my ID and sitting through endless HR videos, I head back around to HR to meet with Kerrie.

"Welcome aboard, Audrey." She smiles and I'm pretty sure I'm smiling just as brightly as her. "You're going to love it here, and I'm confident you'll fit right in. Let me do the final tour of the place, then you can meet Bas and I can let you loose. You can work your magic and find us the next best-selling author."

"That's the plan."

On the tour, we drop my things off in my office, yep, *my* office, and then she shows me around. She shows me to the copy room, break room, meeting rooms, and finally, she takes me to meet the big boss, Bas Blackstone. I know most people would Google stalk their new employer, but I'm not like that. I'm here to do a job. I did stalk the company before I reached out to them, and from what I saw online, I liked their morals and thought it would be a great place to work. It also helps that some of their clients are some of my all-time favorite authors. It will be hard not to fangirl if they ever come into the office.

We head to a corner office with imposing double

wooden doors. Kerrie knocks, and a muffled voice calls out, "Enter."

She pushes on the door, and we step into Bas's office. It's your typical CEO office with a desk and seating area. The building faces Lake Michigan, and the view out the window is to die for. It takes my breath away. How the big boss gets any work done is beyond me, and then I see him. He lifts his head and our gazes catch.

My eyes widen.

My heart stops, and my vagina, well, the hussy starts to throb, because holy fucking shit, it's him—Bastian. My one—no, two—night stand.

"Bas, I'd like to introduce you to Audrey McKeown, our new fiction editor."

We silently stare at one another. Somehow, I manage to find my words and speak, "Mr. Blackstone, it's a pleasure to meet you." My tone is professional, amazingly, but on the inside, I'm a screaming and quivering mess. And not in the orgasmic way I previously did with him. This time it's in fear and shock.

He looks just as shocked as I am, and I plead with my eyes for him not to say anything. He smirks, and fuck me, it's sexy as all hell. *Down, vagina,* I reprimand it, but really, I can't blame her. I'm accosted with a memory of seeing said sexy smirk when he lifted his head from between my thighs after giving me the best oral I've ever had in my life.

"The pleasure is all mine, Ms. McKeown. Lainey and Kerrie have been raving about you all week."

"We've got a winner here," Kerrie adds.

"I trust your judgment, Kerrie." He pushes his chair back from his desk. He walks around it and toward me. He offers me his hand, but for a few moments, I just stand here and stare at it. Then, on autopilot, I lift mine and place it in his.

Like the first time we touched, a spark zaps from him to me. My breath hitches in the back of my throat, and the asshole smirks. *Bastard.*

"Welcome aboard," he says after our "moment." "But if you ladies will excuse me, I have a meeting across town."

"Of course," Kerrie says.

"I hope to see you around, Ms. McKeown," he says.

"Y-y-y-you too," I manage to stammer.

Kerrie and I exit Bastian's office, and we wrap up my tour. We say our goodbyes, and when we part ways, I'm in a fog. Somehow, I make my way back to my office. I fall into my seat, but I just sit here and stare blankly at my computer screen.

This cannot be happening. This is not a novel, this is real life. I can't be working at the same place as my one-night stand, because we all know how that ends up. She gets screwed, literally and figuratively, before getting her happily ever after with the billionaire CEO, but this is real life. It's not fiction, but holy shit, what a happy ending it would be. My two nights with Bastian were hotter than hot, but it was just a moment—well, two moments.

The phone on my desk rings, startling me. I stare at the ringing device and wonder how I should answer. I forgot to ask about that, but I can't leave it unanswered. Reaching out, I pick it up and decide to answer with my name, "Audrey McKeown."

"Drey, it's Bas."

My eyes widen, and I sit up straight. "Mr. Black-stone, what can I, umm, ahh, do for you?"

"You can meet me in my office at six tonight."

"I don't think that's appropriate," I tell him. My heart is racing, and then I start to wonder if he's going to fire me. I remember reading about a nonfraterniza-tion policy in all the documents I just signed, but surely that doesn't apply to dalliances before employment.

"It's just a boss and an employee having a meeting."

"I ... I don't think we should meet in private."

"You worried you'll throw yourself at me again?"

"I beg your pardon, if memory serves correctly, you pursued me. Both times."

"Semantics," he says with an arrogant tone.

"Look, Bastian—"

"Everyone calls me Bas," he interrupts.

"Bastian," I place emphasis on his first name. "I'm here to do a job. I ... I don't need drama in the workplace."

"Who said there would be drama?"

"How can there not be?" I throw back at him, but before he can reply, I keep going. "Blackstone Publishing has a nonfraternization policy, and as the CEO, you, of all people, should follow the rules. I say we pretend that each of us doesn't know what the other looks like naked and we focus on business and business only."

"Babe, there is no way in hell I can forget about you naked. Or the sounds you make when you come, or how fucking sexy you look on your knees as I shove my cock down your throat. That is just not going to happen."

"Well, that's too bad for you, Bastian. Now, if you'll excuse me, I have work to do."

Before he can say anything else, I hang up. It immediately rings again, but I ignore it. This happens three more times, and on the fourth time, I lift up the receiver and place it down on my desk. I can hear Bastian shouting down the line, and I can't help but smirk. Eventually, it goes quiet, and when I pick up the receiver, I realize that he hung up. *Score one for me*, I think to myself.

Leaning back in my chair, I look around my office. This is everything I've ever dreamed of, and I will not let the sexy bastard who is Bastian Blackstone ruin this for me.

13

BASTIAN

My eyes nearly popped out of my head when I looked up and saw Drey standing there. For a moment, I thought I was dreaming, but when Kerrie said, "… Audrey McKeown, our new fiction editor," I knew I was not. Then I was knocked on my ass when she pretended not to know me with her sweet, "Mr. Blackstone, it's a pleasure to meet you," bullshit.

This is something I would pull if I didn't want to associate with a woman I had previously hooked up with, but then again, this woman *is* me.

After her sneaking out, again, a few weeks ago, I have not been able to stop thinking about her. And now I'm imagining fucking her against the windows here in my office like we did in New York. Actually, if Kerrie weren't here, I would bend her over my desk and fuck her. *Makes mental note to make that happen.*

Somehow, I remain professional, and all too soon,

she and Kerrie leave my office. Dropping back into my chair, I shake my head. What are the odds that my mystery woman would be our new fiction editor? Explains why she was reading a manuscript in Bin 501 the first two times I met her.

Leaning back, I wonder if I'm so wrapped up in this woman because she's making me work for it. I do all right with the ladies, and usually they're throwing their panties at me, but Audrey McKeown has made me work for it each time our paths have crossed.

Maybe this is fate's way of apologizing and she's giving me a third shot, like third time lucky, when it comes to this beguiling woman.

Pushing aside thoughts of another chance with Drey, I try to get back to work, but I can't focus. All I seem to keep thinking about is *her*. Knowing that we need to address this, I pick up my phone and dial her office. She answers straightaway, and just the sound of her voice has my cock coming to life in my pants. We bicker, she refuses my meeting request, and then she hangs up on me.

Staring at the phone in my hand, I shake my head. After verbally sparring with her, my cock is rock fucking hard. I dial her number again, but it rings out. I try a few more times, and finally, she picks up, but I'm met with silence. Then I hear a clunk, and I realize she's placed the receiver down on her desk.

"I know you can hear me, Drey," I growl. *Who the*

fuck is this woman? "You will meet with me, and that's a fact," I hiss before I hang up in frustration.

If she thinks I'm going to just walk away without having her again, she's sorely mistaken. I always get what I want, and I want Audrey McKeown. Game on, Drey, game fucking on.

14

———

AUDREY

THE NEXT WEEK passes by quickly, and each day is a repeat of the day before. Bastian calls to request a meeting, but I decline.

He sends me an email meeting request, which I decline. Unless it's a meeting with other people, I will never meet with this man alone. I don't trust myself around him.

On the Wednesday of my second week, he sent me a beautiful bouquet of flowers. The attached note had three words.

You + Me = Dinner

Plucking out the card, I grab my pen and add my answer to the card. Then I pick up the flowers and make my way around to his office.

"That's a lovely bouquet," his assistant, Ms. Ruthven, says when she spots me.

"And they're for you," I tell her.

"Why?"

"Because everyone deserves flowers," I tell her.

"Is Mr Blackstone in?"

"He's out for a meeting but should be back shortly."

"Mind if I drop something on his desk?"

"Not at all." She waves me in, and I drop my reply to his dinner invitation on his desk.

You + Me = Dinner

No!!!

Smirking to myself, I exit his office, wishing I could see the look on his face when he gets my answer, but it does put me in a good mood for the rest of the day.

The next day, a box of my favorite chocolates arrives with another card, but this time it only has one word written on it in his handwriting.

Please?

Grabbing the chocolates, I drop them off in the lunchroom and take the card to his office with my reply.

~~PLEASE?~~

Thanks, but no thanks.

After a weekend spent hurkle-durkling, aka lounging in bed all day, it's time for work again. When I walk into my office, I stop mid-step and my mouth drops open at what I see. There must be at least fifteen different flower arrangements and several boxes of chocolates. Each with their own card asking me to dinner but each card is worded differently. Hell, there's even a "Will you go to dinner with me?" with a YES/NO tick box, reminding me of what you'd send to the person you liked in elementary school.

Dropping my bag in my drawer, I collect all the cards, and like I've done the last two times, I tell him no. On the YES/NO tick box one, I cross out *yes* and add a big tick next to *no*—circling it for good measure.

Placing the chocolates in the lunchroom, I distribute the flowers to my fellow colleagues. Everyone is trying to guess who my admirer is, but I shrug them off, playing dumb.

My most favorite delivery of the morning is dropping off a single sunflower and box of chocolates on *his* desk ... along with *all* the rejection cards.

Chuckling to myself, I head back to my office and get to work. I'm in the final negotiations with Poppy Parson's regarding her novel that I've been devouring.

It's a spicy enemies-to-lovers workplace romance about two childhood sweethearts who are now working together. They are butting heads at every turn, and when they give in to their desires? Holy melted panties. This woman has a way with words when it comes to getting down and dirty, but what I love the most about the book is the love these two have for one another. It's so deep and goes beyond the physical and delves into the emotional connection between them. I'm waiting for each of them to get over the past and move into the "ahh ha" moment. It almost feels like life imitating art.

Animosity, check.

Quick-witted barbs, check.

Sexual tension, check—except we are not fucking like rabbits like the characters in Poppy's book, and we never will again.

I keep glancing up, hoping to see Bastian standing in the doorway, but I don't. Shocking me, I'm disappointed that I didn't see him. I was expecting a retaliation after gifting him one of his flowers, but nothing.

That night in my dreams, however, I dreamed of Bastian marching into my office and pleasuring me with chocolates I dropped off. I woke up like a dog in heat and had to pleasure myself with my trusty vibrator. It was *his* name passing through my lips as I reached my release. This is something that's been a nightly occurrence since I started at Blackstone Publishing. At the rate I'm going, I'll need a new vibrator by the end of the month, but I'm totally placing blame on Poppy and her amazing novel, not *him*.

A few days later, there's a knock at my door, and when I look up, Bastian is standing there. His hands are thrust in his pockets. I can't read his expression, and I'm nervous.

Neither of us speaks.

He just stands there, staring, while I sit here glaring back at him.

I'm not going to be the one to make the first move, but the silence and building sexual tension becomes too much, and I snip, "What can I do for you, Mr. Blackstone?"

"It's Bas," he calmly utters. He steps into my office, closing the door behind him. He leans against it and slips his hand behind him, the sound of the lock clicking echoes around the room. What's normally a spacious office, suddenly feels small and confined. "And since you won't meet with me, I've decided to meet with you."

My lips lift into a smug smile, because I realize I've gotten to him, and I hold all the cards right now. But for the life of me, I don't know which one to play. Schooling my inner turmoil, I flick my eyes from him to the chair in front of my desk and back again.

Nodding, he pushes off the door, and rather than taking the seat across from me, he walks around my desk and perches on the edge next to me. His looming presence towers over me. With one move, he now has all the power. *Bastard.*

Crossing my arms, I lean back in my chair and notice Bastian is looking at my chest. My movement has pushed my tits up, and my usually demure shift dress has now become a cleavage-filled, not-appropriate-for-work dress. Lowering my arms, I stare up at the smirking asshole.

"What can I do for you, Mr. Blackstone?"

"For starters," he growls, "you can cut the Mr. Blackstone bullshit."

"What should I call you then?"

"Bas, like everyone else does."

"But I'm not everyone else," I throw back at him.

"You certainly aren't, Ms. McKeown, and that's one of the reasons I wanted to meet with you. We need to discuss our relationship."

"We do not have a relationship, Mr. Blackstone." His jaw clenches when I say his name like that.

"Ohh, but we do."

"Fucking twice does not make a relationship."

"It was more than twice. It was *several* times. And from memory, we have a very good connection."

"Semantics—" I spit out, and his lips lift into a small smile since he said the same thing to me last week.

"Touché." He crosses his arms and stares down at me.

"Connection aside, it will never happen again, Mr.

Blackstone. And in case you forgot, there's a nonfraternization policy here. I did point this out the other day, but it seems your ego thinks you're above company policy."

"I am the company," he cockily replies.

"And therefore, you, of all people, should abide by said policy."

He stares down at me. It's intense and it's taking everything I have not to throw myself at him, but I would be a hypocrite if I did, especially with what I just told him. "Did you want something?"

"I want you."

"Well, we can't always get what we want. Now, if you'll excuse me, I have a job to do."

"That's no way to speak to your employer."

"And hitting up your employee for sex isn't very professional either."

"Not once did I mention sex."

"Ugh," I hiss, throwing my hands up. "What do you want from me?" He opens his mouth, but I place my hand up to stop him. "And you better not say me. This is a place of business, and we need to keep it professional."

"Then have dinner with me."

"You have dinner with all your employees?"

"No," he steadfastly says.

"Then no. You will treat me like any other employee."

"I haven't fucked any other employee against the

windows of a hotel room, therefore, you are *nothing* like my other employees."

"Well, that's too bad for you, Mr. Blackstone. So, unless you have anything businesswise to discuss, there's the door."

"I'm not going anywhere."

"Fine," I snap. "I'll go."

Pushing my chair back, I stand up, and when I go to walk away, he grabs my wrist and backs me up against the shelves behind my desk. He presses his body into mine. I can feel every muscular ridge and another muscle that's hard and pressing into my stomach. "You and I *will* discuss this," he snarls between clenched teeth.

"There's nothing to discuss. You're my boss. End of story."

"Then you're fired."

"And I'll sue you for unfair dismissal and sexual misconduct."

"It's not misconduct if you want it, and you did want it."

"Did. Past tense." But even as I say that, I know I'm lying. If he weren't my boss, I would totally pursue something with this man, but he *is* my boss. Therefore what my vagina wants is moot. "Please, Bastian," I beg, "let me go."

"I will never take a woman by force, but, Drey, this isn't over. Finding you in my office last week was a shock, but I also think it's fate's way of telling us that there's more to us than just a random hookup."

"You believe in fate?"

"Yes, don't you?"

"I'm a romance editor, what do you think?"

"So why are you fighting us then?"

"Because this is real life, Bastian. I need this job, and your policy prevents us"—I flick my finger back and forth between us—"from ever happening."

"Fuck the policy."

"Bastian," I plead again. "We can't."

"That's not a word that I'm fond of, and I will never push someone to do something they don't want, but mark my words, you and I *will* happen, Audrey."

"While I'm an employee at Blackstone Publishing, that's not going to happen. I may have only been here for a week, but I like it here, and I know I can do great things here. If you care for me, as you say you do, you won't get in the way of that."

With that said, I slip out from under his arm, and, with a racing heart, I unlock my office door and make my way to the restrooms.

Walking into a stall, I lock the door, lower the lid, and sit down. Breathing heavily, I shake my head. That man is going to be the death of me, but I have to remain strong. I just hope I can stay strong, because there is something about Bastian Blackstone that has me questioning every-thing ... and really wanting to break the rules.

15

BASTIAN

...two months later

IT'S BEEN eight long weeks since I found Audrey in my office, and she's still playing hard to get. She declines every meeting request I send, and whenever I send her flowers or chocolates, now only on Fridays, she gives them to someone else in the office—mainly my assistant, Ms. Ruthven. But I have to admit, the look on her face when Audrey gives them to her is a highlight of my week. It's made me realize, I don't appreciate my assistant enough. I make a mental note to do more for her. She really is a life saver, and I would be screwed without her yelling at me to keep me in line.

We've just had our monthly meeting, and for only being here for a short period of time, Audrey is flourishing. "Ms. McKeown," I call out when the meeting ends, "can I have a word, please?"

"Uhh oh, you're in trouble," Lainey teases Audrey, and everyone else chuckles.

Sending me a death glare, Audrey leans back in her chair and crosses her arms. She's once again wearing a dress that with a cross of her arms takes it from office chic to sexy as fuck. She notices where my eyes are staring and quickly uncrosses her arms.

"What can I do for you, Mr. Blackstone?"

"How many times do I have to tell you, my friends call me Bas."

"And how many times do I have to tell you, I'm not your friend. I'm your employee."

"Why won't you give me a chance?"

"Because there's a policy here that strictly forbids us from doing anything, and I actually happen to love my job here. Don't get me wrong, I enjoyed my nights with you, too, but I need to pay my bills."

"You can't be with me and pay your bills?"

"No, there's a policy, and before you even suggest it, I will not quit and become your personal sex slave."

"I wasn't going to suggest that, but I do like the idea of having you as my sex slave."

"Luckily for you, dreams are free. Now, do you have something to actually discuss with me?"

"I wanted to say how impressed I've been with your work ethic. You're the first one here and the last one to leave. You've only been here for a short period of time, and you've already brought in four new authors. I hear you're pursuing a few others too, and are also in final negotiations with another."

"Thank you, and I am. I'm flying to New York early next week to meet with Poppy in person, hoping I can get her to sign on the dotted line. She's an amazing writer, and I think she will be happy here at Blackstone Publishing."

Hmmmm, she's going to New York, I think to myself.

"Well, good luck with that, and just know, whenever you feel like breaking the rules, you know where to find me."

"I'll keep that in mind, but just know, I'm not the rule-breaking type so I'd suggest, you find another woman to woo."

"I don't need or want another woman. My hand and I will be fine until you come to your senses."

"You'll be waiting forever, Mr. Blackstone, but I wish you and Mrs. Palmer all the very best." Without another word, she grabs her things and walks out of the conference room.

My eyes watch her walk away, and I let out a frustrated groan when I'm alone. "You tapping that?" a voice says from behind me, and when I turn around, I see my brother standing there.

"No," I snap.

"Someone needs to get laid," he teases, walking into the room and dropping into a chair next to me.

"Tell me about it," I agree and sit back down. "She's my fuck and duck girl."

"No fucking way, and you hired her?"

"Lainey and Kerrie did. I had no idea until she walked into my office on her first day."

"So, why haven't you fucked her again?"

"I've been trying, but she keeps refusing to go out with me."

"Ohh, I like this girl," my brother unhelpfully states. "You know, I think she's the first girl who hasn't dropped her panties for you."

"She has ... twice ... but now those things are fucking glued on."

"So, woo her."

"I've been trying. Flowers. Chocolates. Nothing seems to work, all because of the nonfraternization policy."

"So, change the policy," he says, as if it's that easy. "You do own the company after all."

"Yeah, but if I change it and then start banging my new editor, I'm just as slimy and sleazy as Chad."

"You are nothing like that asshole. Don't ever compare yourself to that asshat again. The fact that you're respecting her wishes shows that."

"Yeah, but if she said yes, I'd have had her naked and be balls deep inside her before you can say nonfraternization policy."

"So, you're kinda screwed then," he states. "Just not in the naked, fun way, but you know what I mean."

"As much as this has been enlightening, what can I do for you?"

"Volderwhore just tried to gain access to the building."

"What the hell for?"

"She's broke."

"The fuck? She got like a gazillion dollars when you finalized the divorce."

"Don't know and don't care."

"How do you know she's broke?"

"She came to the office the other day and played the 'we should get back together' card. An—"

"You're not, are you?"

"Fuck no. That ship has sailed ... and sunk. Plus, I'm happy with Suzanne." And when he says he's happy, he means it. I've never seen Beau like this before, and it's all because of Suzanne. She is his other half, and I have high hopes that he's finally found his penguin. "I guess she thought trying to seduce me at home was her next step 'cause she was there in a trench coat and heels."

"That's an image I didn't need."

"We can suffer together," he throws back at me. "I should be fine now. I've filed a restraining order against her so if she tries again, I'll leave it to the police."

"Fingers crossed this is the end of Volderwhore."

Conversation turns to what we've been up to recently, since he and I haven't really hung out lately, but we do make arrangements to have dinner later tonight. Just before he leaves, he gives me some free legal advice and reminds me that I'm the boss and I can change policies with board approval.

He heads out and I sit here, pondering his words, because he's right. I can do what I want with *my* company, but before I make any changes, I need to make sure she's what I want. As I pack up my things, I start making plans for a trip to New York.

16

———

AUDREY

Iᴛ's Friday and I'm in a mood. I'd blame it on PMS, but that was last week. No, I'm pissed off because of none other than Bastian Blackstone. Bastian, affectionately known to me as Bastard Blackstone, has ignored me since the meeting the other day.

He's.

Ignored.

Me.

I'm pissed he's giving me the cold shoulder, but most of all, I'm pissed at myself for being pissed that he's not wooing me. It's illogical and doesn't make sense, but then again, nothing with that bastard does.

It's nearly quitting time, and this is the first Friday I've not received anything from him. Maybe he's finally gotten the hint, but why does that thought gut me? There's a knock at my door, and when I look up, the bastard in question is standing in my doorway. "Do you have plans this evening?"

"I'm not having dinner with you," I hiss at him.

"I wasn't here to ask you to dinner."

"Ohhh," I dejectedly reply and once again, I'm pissed with myself for being upset that he didn't ask me out.

"So, do you have plans?" he asks again.

"No, I don't," I tell him. I thought about lying to him, but I'm not a liar and I don't want to play games with him.

"You do now," he emphatically states. "You and I are going to attend a charity gala."

"What?" I hiss, shocked at what he just said—well, commanded.

"Beau's company holds a charity gala once a year, and you are going as my date."

"I ... what?"

He stares at me. "You plus me equals—"

"No," I interrupt him.

"It's not a suggestion, Ms. McKeown. You *will* be my date this evening."

"Or what?"

"Or I will send Lainey to New York next week to woo Poppy Parsons."

"Oh my God, you..."

"Me what?" he growls, but why he's angry, I don't know. I'm the one who deserves to be pissed.

"Just because I won't sleep with you again does not mean you can undermine me like that." What he did just now is unacceptable on so many levels. "Your parents messed up when you were born, they spelt Bastian wrong on your birth certificate, it should be B-A-S-T-A-R-D."

"Did you just call me a bastard?"

"If the shoe fits," I snap at him, and now I really wish I did lie. Spending an evening with him is the last thing I want to do. *Liar.*

He smiles at me in a way that both infuriates and turns me on. "Call me whatever you like, sweetheart, but you will be my date this evening. I'll have a car pick you up at seven."

Silently we stare at one another. Him gloating and me fuming. Poppy is my client, and it *will* be *me* going to New York on Monday, so I smile nicely at the bastard. "Well, if you don't mind, my bastard of a boss has just demanded I attend a function tonight, and I need to go get a dress and get ready. I refuse to let him make a fool of me."

"I'm sure Bastard would be happy to let you leave early." He grins in that sexy infuriating way, living up to his bastard monicker I've given him. "Go and see Sophie at Maxton's. She'll get you sorted."

"I'm perfectly capable of finding my own dress," I snap.

"I know you are, but since this is last minute, allow me to cover the expenses."

"Fine," I concede, but we both know I'm not really

conceding because Maxton's is a really nice and expensive boutique. I've always wanted to shop there, but my budget does not extend that far.

"Excellent," he replies. "I'll let Sophie know you're on your way."

"Fine," I mumble.

"I'll pick you up at seven," he confirms again.

"Fine," I grumble. I can see him getting pissed at me repeating the same word again and again, and it's hard to not smirk in glee, but it's good to know I affect him as much as he affects me.

"This is the one," Sophie beams, clapping her hands in delight, but she's right. I'm wearing a mid-length strapless dress in an eggnog-tone with butterfly embellishments and a lace-up back. It's sexy without being overly flirty, and the color complements my skin tone and hair perfectly.

"Mr. Blackstone will be very pleased," she coos, and hearing that pisses me off. This is for me, not for him, but the thought of him losing his mind over something he can't have has me grinning from ear to ear.

"It really is gorgeous," I agree with her as I do a little spin on the podium. With my dress and shoes sorted, I head home, and when I arrive, I find a makeup artist and hairstylist waiting for me in the lobby.

We head upstairs, and when we enter my apartment, I quickly shower and then I'm transformed from office worker to sophisticated gala attendee.

Not long after they leave, Jeff, the doorman calls up, letting me know Bastian is here. Not wanting to let him into my apartment, I tell him I'm on my way down.

Checking my lipstick one more time, I grab my clutch and head out. Locking my door, I walk down the corridor to the elevators. Pushing the button, I wait, and when it arrives, I step in and the metal car whisks me down to the ground floor. The doors open, and before I exit, I check my reflection one last time and smile. I really do look stunning tonight.

Taking a deep breath, I step out into the lobby, but I pause mid step when my gaze lands on Bastian. He's chatting with Jeff and hasn't noticed me yet, so I take a moment to check him out.

My eyes roam over his midnight-black tuxedo clad body. He can wear the fuck out of a suit in the office, but in a tuxedo? He's utterly dashing. His hair is gelled back, and when he turns to face me, my breath hitches in the back of my throat. Holy sex on a stick, this man has literally taken my breath away.

"Audrey," he utters my name and heads in my direction. The sound of those six letters passing through his lips washes over me in a way like never before. "You are exquisite." He stops before me and brushes a tendril of hair behind my ear. His fingertips gently graze my cheek, and it leaves a heated trail in their path. He stares intently at me, and I'm not sure how I feel about all this attention.

"Thank you," I shyly reply, dropping my gaze from his. The intensity of his stare is too much. I need a moment, but my moment is short-lived when he grips my chin between his thumb and forefinger and lifts my head up. "Don't hide your pretty face from me."

"I wasn't hiding," I tell him, shaking my head. "I..." But I don't know what to say. I don't want him to know he's affecting me, but from the smug grin on his face, he already knows.

"Shall we?" He offers me his elbow.

Nodding, I slide my hand into the crook of his arm, and together we exit my building and head out to the waiting limo. The driver opens the door, and I nod my thanks to him before I climb in.

When Bastian slides into the seat next to me, my heart begins to race. His nearness causes my heart to beat even faster. *What is happening?* I think to myself as the car pulls out into traffic.

"Champagne?" he asks, and I nod. Words are hard right now. Thinking about the word *hard* has my gaze dropping to his crotch, but when I realize what I'm doing, I avert my eyes. Turning my head, I stare out the window, watching the buildings fly by.

"Here," he utters, and I turn to face him. He hands

me a glass of bubbly. Our eyes lock. He smiles and then makes a toast. Raising his glass, he looks over at me. "To finding you again and a great night."

"To a great night," I repeat, because finding me is inconsequential. Even as I think that, I don't believe a word I just refuted because I have a feeling him finding me again will be the best thing to ever happen to me.

17

BASTIAN

When I looked up and saw Audrey standing in the lobby, I smiled because I have never seen a more beautiful woman in all my life. She's sexy in an understated way. The fact she doesn't even realize how stunning she is makes her even sexier, and the dress she chose, fuck me, it's perfectly her.

I was disappointed when the doorman told me she was on her way down, I wanted to see her apartment. In hindsight, I'm glad that didn't happen because when she opened the door and my eyes landed on hers, I would have pushed her back into her apartment, and we wouldn't have made it to the event.

After idle chatter and a drink, our car arrives at The Geraghty. Climbing out first, I turn and offer my hand to Audrey. She looks at it, then at me, and then back at her hand. "It's just a hand," I tell her.

"Yeah, *your* hand," she replies, but she places hers

in mine and I help her out of the car. Dropping her hand, I slide my arm around her waist and rest my palm on her lower back.

Together, we walk up the red carpet and into the building. Like I always do, I ignore the calls of the reporters. Paparazzi are the scum of the earth, but I won't make a scene. It's not my style. Plus, tonight is about charity, and Beau would kill me if I did anything to detract from that.

We enter the building and, like always, I'm amazed when I step inside. They did a great job restoring this place. In its former days, it was a paper mill, but today, it's a sophisticated event space with endless possibilities.

My gaze drifts to Audrey, and I watch as she spins around, her face brightening as she takes in the room. "It's beautiful," she coos.

Stepping over to her, I lean in and whisper, "It is ... and I'm not referring to the building." Pressing my lips just below her ear, I kiss her. Her skin breaks out in goosebumps and her breath hitches. Sliding my arms around her waist, I pull her into me, her back to my front. I press my hardening dick into her ass. "When this thing is over, you are coming back to my place, and I'm going to fuck you all night long—and this time, you and I will have breakfast together. Then I'll take you back to bed and fuck you until it's time for work on Monday."

Her chest rises and falls rapidly. She's just as

turned on as I am. She glances over her shoulder and opens her mouth to reply, but she's interrupted when my cockblocking brother joins us.

"You made it," he says, smirking at me.

"Of course I did," I snap. "I said I'd be here."

Audrey elbows me in the stomach and glowers at me for being rude. The hit causes me to let out an "oomph" from the contact.

"I like her," my brother interjects, grinning like the asshole he is. He turns his attention to Audrey and gives her his toothpaste AD-worthy smile as he takes her hand and kisses her knuckle. "I'm Beau, the better-looking brother."

"Audrey," she replies.

Beau holds her hand for longer than is appropriate, and I'm about to punch him in the face when he finally drops her hand. "Glad you could be here, but I'm sorry you're stuck with him."

"He's not so bad," she replies, and for some unknown reason, hearing her say that has my heart fluttering. *What is this woman doing to me?* "This place is stunning," she tells him.

"It sure is," he agrees, "and as much as I would like to take credit for this, I have little to do with the planning. They just tell me what to do, and I do it."

"Sounds like you have the easy job."

"You might be right. The bar is over there." He nods to the side of the room. "We're at table three. Now, if you'll excuse me, I need to find my date."

"It was lovely to meet you," Audrey tells him.

"You too, Audrey. Save me a dance later, and I can give you all the dirt on my brother."

"Don't make me junk punch you," I growl.

"So touchy, Bas. Sounds like you need to get laid."

"I'm fine," I hiss.

"Mmmhmpf," he says, and before I can say anything, he walks away from Audrey and me.

"He seems nice," she voices when it's just the two of us.

"Mmmhmpf," I utter. "Shall we get a drink?"

She looks to me and smiles. "Let's."

Before I can reply, she heads in the direction of the bar. Standing here, I watch her walk away, and I start to wonder if inviting her here tonight was a good idea after all.

18

AUDREY

"HE DID NOT?" I question Suzanne, Beau's girlfriend and my favorite dirty-martini-making bartender from Bin 501.

"Ohhh, he did." She looks to Beau, and I see nothing but love radiating between the two of them. They make a cute couple. I love how at ease they are with one another. I want that for myself, but as time goes on, I think that it's only going to happen for those around me and for the couples in the books I edit.

"Dance with me?" Bastian demands after the dessert plates are cleared.

Turning to look at him, I glare. He's been surly and rude most of the evening and has hardly spoken a word to me.

"No," I flatly tell him.

He mumbles something under his breath, but it was no doubt snarky. Needing a break, I stand up and push my chair back. Bastian reaches out and grips my wrist. Like every time we touch, a spark jolts through me, but it evaporates when he hisses, "Where are you going?"

"Bathroom. Is that all right with you?

He nods and reluctantly lets my wrist go.

"I'll come too," Suzanne says. She leans over, kisses Beau, and then stands up. We head to the restrooms, and I hear Beau utter, "Why do girls always go in pairs to the ladies' room?"

"I don't know," Bastian snaps. "I'm not a chick."

"You're acting like one," Beau throws back at him, and they start to bicker like children, but then again, Bastian is acting like one.

Thankfully, there's no line and I head straight into a stall. Tonight is not going like I thought it would. I was hoping Bastian and I would have a nice night together, but he's being a snarky bastard.

A giggle escapes me as I think about telling him that this afternoon. From the stall next to me, Suzanne calls out, "Why are you laughing while peeing?"

"I was thinking about a conversation with Bastian this afternoon."

"Why do you call him that?" she asks, and then I hear the toilet flush and her door unlock.

"That's his name," I reply.

Finishing my business, I wipe, flush, and exit. Walking over to the sink, I wash my hands.

"It is, but his friends call him Bas."

"I'm not his friend."

"Well, what are you?" She pauses. "If you don't mind me asking."

"I'm ... no one."

"Could have fooled me. The sexual tension between you two is off the charts. I say fuck him and get it out of your system."

"Didn't work the first two times," I mumble, then my eyes widen when I realize what I just said, and I cover my mouth.

"I knew it," she gleefully singsongs.

"Forget you heard that."

"Uhhh uh." She shakes her head. "You and I are heading to the bar and then you're going to tell me ev-ery-thing."

"I don't have a choice, do I?"

"Nope." She shakes her head. Looping her arm through mine, she guides me out of the restroom and directly to the bar.

"Two shots of whiskey and two champagnes, please," she orders from the barman and looks back at me. "This feels like a shots kind of conversation."

"It really is." I nod in agreement.

The barman places two shots before us and we each pick them up. "Cheers," we both call out and shoot back the whiskey. It burns the whole way down and, thankfully, my glass of bubbly is waiting for me to put out the flames. Picking up my glass, I take a sip and it eases the burn, slightly. "That was nasty."

"But did it give you the courage to tell me?"

"No." I shake my head. She orders two more shots. "It's fine," I tell the barman as I eye Suzanne, but she just laughs. Taking my hand, she walks over to a high-top table and rests her elbows on the top. She looks at me in a "okay, it's story time" kind of way.

Taking a sip of my drink, I fill her in on my and Bastian's escapades since we first met at Bin 501.

"Want my opinion?" she states when I finish telling my story. Nodding, I stare at my new friend and wait for her words of wisdom. "Fuck him one last time and get him out of your system."

"I'm not sure I could forget him."

"Tell me about it," she agrees, and my eyes widen when I realize that she's slept with Bastian.

"You ... you've slept with him?"

"I, ummm, had a threesome with him and Beau one night."

"What?" I hiss. "When?"

"It was ages ago. Before Beau married Volder-whore. It was just the one time, but Bas and I didn't fuck-fuck. Yes, I blew him, and his dick briefly entered my vagina, but he could see the connection between Beau and me, so he let us have all the fun and he just watched."

"If you guys had such a connection, why did he marry that other chick?"

"It wasn't our time," she says with a shrug. "I think we needed the time apart to grow as people. I wouldn't change a thing. I'm happier than I've ever been. For what it's worth, I've never seen Bas so taken with someone."

"But he's my boss."

"So?"

"There's a company policy."

"Ohh, well, then, you have a couple of choices. Fuck the rules and screw him, quit so you can fuck him without consequence, or walk away. But for what it's worth, option three is the wrong one. Life is too short to miss out on good dick, and we both know, that man knows how to wield his dick. And speaking of dick, I'm going to find *my* man and dry hump him on the dance floor so that when we get home later, I get some reeeeeally good dick." She winks at me, walks over to Beau, and drags him out to the dance floor.

"I wish it were that simple," I mumble to myself.

Needing some air, I finish my drink and head toward the doors leading to the outdoor terrace. It's cloudy when I step out onto the terrace, but the fairy lights overhead light the area, creating a romantic atmosphere.

Leaning on the railing, I stare out at the parking lot below and think about what Suzanne said. I do like Bastian, more than I care to admit, but he's my boss and there's the policy. But at the same time, that man fucks like no one I've ever been with before. And when he's not being a bastard, he's actually a great guy.

"There you are," the man in question says.

"I just needed some air," I tell him.

"Everything okay?" Nodding, I bite my lip and drop my gaze to my feet. He eats up the distance between us. I see his feet before me, and like he has a habit of doing, he places his fingertip under my chin and lifts my head up. He stares intently at me, and before my brain can stop me, I lean in and press my lips to his.

Without missing a beat, he wraps his arms around me and slides his hand up into my hair and kisses me back. His tongue licks into my mouth, and with one tongue lash, I'm under his spell.

Lifting my leg, he wraps it around his waist, and I unabashedly grind myself on his leg. "Please," I whimper into the kiss, and without me voicing what please means, he slips his hand under my dress, shoves my panties to the side, and thrusts his finger into my hot, wet channel.

"Yes," I pant against his lips.

He plunges his finger in and out of me. I grind down on his hand and kiss him harder. Out of nowhere, my orgasm detonates, and I moan into his mouth. He pulls back and once again gazes intently at me. He removes his hand, slips my panties back into place, and then brings his fingers to his lips and licks them clean.

Standing here panting, with my leg wrapped around him, I realize what I just did, and I hate myself for it. Pushing on his chest, he lets go of my leg. "Audrey," he says my name, and it sounds like a plea.

"I ... we shouldn't have done that." Before he can say anything, I race away from him. Heading to our table, I grab my things and exit the event.

Running down the stairs, I thank the heavens when I see a taxi waiting, and I climb into the back seat. I give the driver my address, and just as he begins to pull away, I look up to see Bastian standing at the top of the stairs, staring at me.

Closing my eyes, I lean back in my seat and sigh in frustration. I shouldn't have done that, but fuck me, that was hot. Looks like I added a fourth option to Suzanne's suggestions: dry hump him in the courtyard and let him finger fuck me, fraternization policy be damned. But seriously, I will not jeopardize this job for good dick. I need to get myself under control around him, because no matter what Suzanne says, no dick is worth a job.

Thankfully, I'm heading to New York on Monday. It will give me a few extra days away from Bastian and give me time to come up with a plan on how to stay away from him. Fate, however, is a bitch, and my New York trip doesn't go as I planned—and in the coming months, that trip will change the course of my life.

19

———

BASTIAN

"Fancy meeting you here," I say in greeting as I drop into the first-class seat next to Drey. I can't help but smirk at the look of shock laced with anger on her face.

"For fuck's sake," she mumbles. Then she growls, "What are you doing here?"

"Flying to New York," I nonchalantly reply.

"Why?"

"Business."

"Business," she repeats, "in New York?" I nod. "And you just so happen to be on the same flight as me? And sitting in first class next to me?"

"Small world, huh?" Little does she know, I upgraded her ticket from business to first so we could be next to each other.

"The world is not that small," she snaps. "And I'm here for business."

"And so am I," I tell her, and that's only marginally true. I don't have any Blackstone business in New York, but I am meeting with someone to discuss opening another office in New York. I'm trying to decide between here, Denver, or DC. DC is too political, New York is too busy, and Denver, well, it's home to my favorite hockey team, the Dragons. If I decide there, I can combine work and hockey.

The flight attendant walks past, and I hail her down and order two coffees—a long black for me and an almond milk latte with two sugars for Drey.

"You know my coffee order?"

"Mmmhmpf," I confirm. "I know everything about you, Drey."

"Mmmhmpf." She crosses her arms, and like always when she does that, my gaze drops to her chest. Sue me, I'm a man, but Audrey McKeown has the best tits I've ever seen, or felt. One of these days, I *will* fuck them. I just need to bide my time until I can wear down her defenses. "Okay, Mr. Stalker, what's my favorite color?"

"You don't have one. You like all colors equally." Her eyes widen at me knowing this, and I have to say, shocking her is fast becoming a favorite hobby of mine.

"Favorite flower?"

"Sunflowers. The whole office now likes them, too." This causes her to smile. "But you like them because they're bright and happy."

"Favorite drink?"

"That's an easy one. Martini."

"What type?"

"Dirty." I lean in and whisper, "You are also dirty in the bedroom, against glass windows, and on terraces at The Geraghty."

"Favorite book?"

"Like colors, you don't have an all-time favorite, but you prefer romance over any other genre. And for the record, I really hope you secure Poppy. She has a way with words that's magical, and she sucks you in. Her book is the perfect mix of spice, drama, and emotion."

"You've read it?" she asks, her tone laced with shock.

"I peruse all the manuscripts of our first-time authors and, occasionally, they suck me in, and I can't put them down. And Poppy's was one of those."

"Really?"

"Really, really." I pause. "You seem shocked."

"Because I am, I just didn't think the CEO would care ... or read romance."

"There are many things you don't know about me, Drey. For example, my favorite color is amber, it reminds me of whiskey and is why the company logo is amber. Favorite flower is now a sunflower, and before that, I never had one. Favorite drink is whiskey, preferably Macallan—"

"Neat," she adds.

"Yes, neat. Seems we know quite a lot about one

another. I mean, I know what you sound like when you come on my dick pressed up against a window, and that you look sexy as fuck when you come all over my fingers." Her mouth drops open at my words. "If you don't shut your mouth, I'm going to shut it with my dick."

"You wouldn't dare. We're on a plane."

"Welcome to the Mile-High Club, baby." As soon as the words pass my lips, I cringe. Rule 101 of seduction, never mention other conquests.

"Of course, you're a member."

"You can't tell me you're not?"

"Do I look like the kind of person to do that?"

"I'm not sure, but I know you're the kind of person who likes me to fuck her up against the windows of a hotel room. I should see if I can get that room again, and we can create new memories."

"You and I will never be getting naked together again, Bastian. Now, if you don't mind, I need to prepare for my meeting."

She pulls out her MacBook and opens the lid, but I reach over and slam it shut. "Do you mind?"

"Not at all, but you and I both know you don't need to prepare. You were prepared the same day you locked in this meeting with Poppy, because you, Audrey McKeown, are a go-getter who leaves no I's undotted or T's uncrossed. You can do this meeting blindfolded. You want to know what I think?"

"Not particularly, but you're going to tell me anyway."

"You want me just as much as I want you—"

"Conceited much?" she interrupts with a raised eyebrow.

"Not conceited, just confident in what I know, and I know you want me. The pink tinge to your cheeks and the way you're pressing your thighs together to quell that tingle that's developing between your legs is a dead giveaway."

"I... I..."

"Don't even try to deny it, Drey. Just give in, you know we're great together."

"Just because we had two amazing nights together, doesn't mean I need to give you a third."

"Amazing, huh?"

"Don't try and act aloof, Bastian, it doesn't suit you. You know it was great, and what's killing you the most is that I won't drop my panties and blow you right now. Let's just put the past in the past and move on. Our relationship is now professional, take it or leave it. And for what it's worth, I hope you can respect my wishes, because I love working at Blackstone Publishing. I don't want what happened privately to affect me professionally."

She opens her laptop and slips in her earbuds, effectively ending the conversation.

Sitting back in my seat, I stare at the seat in front of

me and find myself more turned on than ever. I'll let her go, for now, but mark my words, we will be horizontally tangoing again. What shocks me even more is I don't just want to fuck her. I want to get to know her. Seems she has a magical cunt, and I'm under her spell.

20

———

AUDREY

"I'M so glad you decided to sign with us," I tell Poppy as she finishes signing on the dotted line.

"I'm excited too, and I'm glad that my, ummm, personal circumstances didn't change your opinion of me."

"Poppy, we love who we love, and who you love shouldn't impede you professionally." Poppy just told me that she's in a throuple relationship with Colton Bolton from the New York Crushers and another man, Alexander McQueen, son of Maverick "Rick" McQueen, the Crushers' assistant coach.

"Are you sure you don't need to run it by anyone at Blackstone?"

Shaking my head, I smile at my new client. "If anyone has anything to say, they can stick it up their ass, and if they have a problem, they can take it up with me. All I need you to do is to focus on your words and keep writing."

"I like the sound of that. Writing I'm good at, it's the rest I struggle with."

"Well, then, looks like you and I have the beginning of a beautiful relationship. You can focus on the words, I can make your book shine, and our marketing department can take care of the rest. You will also need to do some promotions on your end to keep the flow going, but between all of us, you'll be a USA Today best-seller before we know it."

"From your lips to God's ears."

"Poppy, this book"—I tap the manuscript before me—"is a winner. Even Bastian agrees."

"The owner?" she says with a shriek.

A laugh escapes, and I nod. "Yep, he read it and loved it, just like I did."

"Wow, I, umm, I don't know what to say." Suddenly, she claps her hands. "We need to go out and celebrate."

"You go out and celebrate with your men. Room service, a bottle of wine, Netflix, and a king bed are calling my name."

"That sounds boring," she huffs.

"Boring to you but heaven to me, plus I can charge it to the company."

"Well, I hope you get a bottle of Dom and the filet mignon."

"Tempting, but I'm more of a dirty martini and a burger kind of girl."

"Ohhh, that does sound good, but I'm looking forward to dancing with my men before we go home and, well, you read that scene."

"Which one?"

"All of them."

"Ohhh, to be young and in love."

"You're young," she tells me. "Any man would be lucky to have you. Maybe you need to have a New York fling."

As she says that, my mind drifts back to the last time I was here, and the antics Bastian and I got up to against the window in that hotel room.

"Why do I get the feeling you've already had a New York fling?" Nonchalantly I shrug before I wink at her. "I knew I liked you for a reason. Eventually, I'm going to ply you with dirty martinis, and I'll get the gossip. You never know, it may end up in a book."

"Ohhh, this has been done in plenty of romance novels, but I can unequivocally say, real life is far better."

"Amen, sister."

Poppy and I wrap things up and we part ways. I head back to my hotel and when I enter the lobby, I decide to stop in at the lobby bar for a drink to celebrate. Poppy is going to make it big. I feel it in my bones, and I can't wait to help her achieve her goals and see her succeed.

"Martini, dirty," I order from the bartender as I slide onto a stool. I've been smiling since I left my meeting with Poppy.

My drink is placed in front of me, and before I get a chance to pick it up, a deep voice from beside me drawls, "Fancy meeting you here."

Turning my head, I see Bastian standing there. He's in jeans and a black button-down and, man, that man can rock the casual look.

"Bastian," I say in greeting, and finally, I take a sip. The savory and salty liquid dances over my taste buds, and I moan slightly.

"That sound you make..." He drifts off, not finishing his sentence, but from the heated look in his eyes, I can guess where his mind is at right now. "Whiskey, neat," he orders from the bartender who just returned. "How'd it go with Poppy?"

"Very well," I excitedly tell him, taking another sip, sans moan this time. "She signed on the dotted line and is excited to be working with us but, umm, she was worried about one thing..."

"I'm guessing it's her throuple relationship?"

"You know?"

"I'm friends with Xander's father."

"Of course you are." Is there anyone this man doesn't know? I wouldn't be surprised if he knows the president, or the guys from Metallica.

"What does that mean?"

"Nothing," I defend. Then, I quickly change focus

because I really don't want to ruin the high I'm currently on. "How was your business?" I air quote *business* because I'm still not sure he actually has any business here in New York.

"It didn't go as planned." I see the devastation on his face, and now I feel bad for doubting him and his reason for being here in New York.

"Wanna talk about it?"

"I want to forget about it," he dejectedly sighs. Bringing his tumbler to his lips, he throws back his drink in one gulp. "Another," he states to the barman, who just finished serving a couple beside us. The barman pours him a new drink, and like the first, he throws it back. "Another," he commands.

"No," I cover Bastian's glass, and if looks could kill, I'd be six feet under. "Drinking is not the answer," I tell him, earning myself an eye roll. "You and I are going to go have dinner and talk."

"Are you asking me to dinner?"

"I am, but not in the way you're hoping, it's just dinner."

"We'll see," he cockily says, and I already regret offering to have dinner with him. "Are you ready to go now or should we meet back here later?"

"Now's good," I tell him. I finish my martini, and he settles our tabs. "I know this great little place. Shall we try there?"

"Sure." He nods. He offers me his hand, and we

exit the lobby bar. "Actually, I might drop this off at my room. Do you mind?"

"Not at all."

Nodding, I turn and walk toward the elevators. Racing up to my room, I drop off my work bag and quickly freshen up, for me, not for him. After checking my reflection, I head back down to meet Bastian, and as I walk across the lobby, I take the opportunity to check him out. Bastian Blackstone is an extremely attractive man, and when you put aside his cockiness, he's also a great man. The women in the office respect him, and he shows respect for all who earn it. Whether it be Ray in the mailroom or Sandy at reception, he treats everyone the same. He doesn't make people fear his presence, and in bed? Wow. I still remember what it felt like when he slid into me. That memory will be with me for the rest of my life.

Shaking off those thoughts, I think about anything other than his dick, but when I reach him and he turns to face me, all my PG thoughts evaporate, along with my panties ... I'm in trouble.

21

———

BASTIAN

THE ELEVATOR DINGS, the sound echoes across the lobby, and when I look up and see Drey exit, my dick likes what I see. *Down, boy.* This woman is the perfect package. She's fucking stunning, but she's no blonde bimbo. She's intelligent, has a sharp mind, and a wicked tongue ... and I'm not just talking about when it's wrapped around my dick. *I wonder if I can get that to happen tonight?* She's adamant that it won't, but I know she feels what I feel. I just need to get her to admit it, and I'm up for the challenge.

"Ready?" she offers when she reaches me.

Nodding, I step aside and offer for her to go first. It's the gentlemanly thing to do, and it's not my fault if it also gives me an unobstructed view of her delectable ass and legs. She's wearing a figure-hugging dress and fuck-me heels. I'm imagining her in nothing but her heels as I fuck her from behind ... against the windows in my room.

Shaking off those thoughts, I focus on her and the night ahead.

The restaurant she suggested was amazing. The food and wine were delicious, and the company was perfect. The more time I spend with Audrey, the more I want her, but no matter how hard I try, she ignores my advances and changes the topic whenever I take it a step too far.

We're sitting out on the sidewalk, and I've just settled the bill—after arguing over who is paying. We're enjoying the last of our wine when a deep voice from the street growls, "Well, well, well, what the fuck do we have here?" When I lift my head in the direction of the voice, my eyes widen when I see Chad Hastings standing there. I see nothing but pure hatred in his gaze, which is directed at me.

"Hello, Chad," I say to the angry man who is now beside us.

"Don't fucking *hello Chad* me, you piece of shit. You ruined my life. My career."

"I beg your pardon?" I snap at him.

"You're fucking her." He thrusts his thumb in Audrey's direction.

"Audrey and I do not have a sexual relationship."

"Then why are you two on a date here in New York?"

"Not that it's any of your business, but we're both here on business."

"Yeah, I know what kind of business you do. One of these days, you're going to mess up, and I'll be there to laugh in your face at your downfall."

"It was nice seeing you, Chad. Now if you'll excuse us, we have an early flight in the morning."

Without saying a word, I stand up and help Audrey to her feet. Thankfully, a cab has just dropped off some late diners, and the two of us climb in. Giving the driver the hotel name, I sit back and sigh.

"Who was that?" Audrey asks as the driver pulls out into traffic.

"Chad Hastings, he was the old editorial editor."

"What's his problem?"

"He was let go for sleeping with an intern."

Her eyes widen at that revelation, and I can see her mind running. "You and I have not done anything wrong. We slept together before you started, and nothing happened at The Geraghty." She eyes me. "Well, okay, something did but that was all me, and you have nothing to worry about."

"Clearly I do. That man was so angry."

"Nothing is going to happen to you, Audrey, I promise."

"You can't promise me that, but for what it's worth, I'm a big girl and I can look after myself."

"I'm sure you can, but if you should happen to run into Chad again, please let me know. I don't want anything to happen to you."

"I promise," she agrees, just as the cab pulls up to the hotel.

We head into the hotel, and I reach out to grab her hand. "Would you join me for a nightcap?"

"I ... umm. I really shouldn't."

"It's just a drink," I tell her. She stares at me and eventually she nods.

"One drink," she states.

"One drink," I confirm, and we head into the lobby bar for "one drink."

22

AUDREY

"Ugh, my head," I groan and then my eyes fly wide open when I realize I'm naked and there's a hard body snuggling into me from behind. Cautiously, I turn my head, and my eyes widen when I see Bastian beside me.

Closing my eyes again, I count to five and open them again, hoping that it was just a dream, but it's not. "Fuck. Fuck. Fuck," I hiss.

"We did," a deep sleep riddled voice murmurs from beside me. "Many times," he adds.

"What?" I ask, as I shimmy around to face Bastian. In the early morning light, with sleep-tousled hair, he looks even more gorgeous.

"We fucked many, many times last night."

"What?" I screech and instantly I regret it. My head is pounding. My mouth feels like the bottom of a dirty ashtray and my vagina, she's swollen and throbbing. Closing my eyes, I enjoy the darkness, and then my eyes snap open. "Why am I only wearing my heels?"

"You don't remember?"

Shaking my head, I groan at the sudden movements. "The last thing I clearly remember is walking into the lobby bar for a nightcap."

"We had several different nightcaps down there and then—"

"Ohh, shit. I remember now."

One dirty martini led to an espresso martini. An espresso martini led to a Brandy Alexander, and that led to a kiss, a not-suitable-for-the-lobby-bar type kiss. That led to trouble, because seconds later, we exited the bar, hand in hand. Then we were in the elevator heading up to his room, dry humping like teenagers. We stumbled out of the elevator and down the corridor to his room, which I realized was next to mine.

As soon as the door to his room clicked shut, it was a race to strip off everything but my shoes.

"I want to fuck you in your shoes," he demanded when I bent down to remove them.

"How do you want me?" I seductively asked.

"Rest your hands on the edge of the sofa and put your ass out."

"So bossy," I teased as I bent over and looked at him

over my shoulder. He was gripping his cock, gently stroking himself. "That's hot," I told him.

"No, seeing you bent over like that is hot, but you know what will be hotter?"

"What?" I desperately panted.

"My cock sliding in and out of your cunt while you play with your tits and clit."

"Well, what are you waiting for?"

"I'm waiting for you to play with your tits and clit."

"Like this?" I purred.

Standing back up, I spun around and rested my naked ass on the arm of the sofa. My hands went to my chest, and I squeezed my tits before pulling on my nipples. Leaving one hand on my breasts, I slid the other down to my slit and circled the pad of my finger over my clit. "Fuuuuuck," I moaned, it was sensation overload. Him stroking himself. Me tugging on my tits. My finger on my clit. It was arousal overload, and I was close to combusting.

"Do not come," he growled, as if he sensed I was on the edge.

"Or what?"

"Or I'll spank you."

"That doesn't seem like a punishment to me."

"You dirty, dirty girl."

"You seem surprised."

"To be honest, yes. I wasn't expecting you to be so..."

"So what?"

"You."

"Thank you, I think."

"Definitely a compliment. Now move your hand. It's time for me to fuck you."

"Oh my God," I cry out as the memories of last night come back to me in all their sexy, Technicolor glory.

"You screamed that a few times last night, too, if I remember correctly," he cheekily says from next to me.

"Please stop. I'm embarrassed enough."

"Why are you embarrassed, Drey? Last night was amazing, unexpected, but amazing."

"I ... we can't keep doing this. You're the boss. There's the clause." I pause, "Shit, I'm going to get fired."

"You are not going to get fired, Drey."

"How do you know?"

"Because I'm the boss."

23

———————

BASTIAN

"Because I'm the boss. And as your boss, I think we should do it again."

"As your employee, for now, I think you're fucking crazy." She hesitantly adds the "for now' part and I hate seeing fear etched on her beautiful face. "This cannot and will not happen again. You're my boss, end of story."

"I could fire you like you suggested, and then I could fuck you, if that's easier on your conscience."

"No," she screeches, sitting up. "I don't want you to fire me, and I certainly don't want to have sex with you again."

"Your perky nipples and flushed cheeks state otherwise."

She looks down and realizes her breasts are showing. She reaches out and pulls the sheet up, covering her chest.

"I'm not aroused, I'm ... I'm embarrassed," she snaps.

"So, your nipples get hard when you're embarrassed?"

"No, that's the AC. Now, if you'll excuse me, I need to go."

She climbs out of bed, keeping the sheet wrapped around her. She bends down to pick up her clothes and enters the bathroom, closing the door behind her. A few moments later, she reemerges dressed in yesterday's outfit, and without a word, she exits my room. The sound of the lock engaging echoes through the room.

This isn't the morning I envisioned last night, but at least she didn't sneak out this time, that's a bonus.

Climbing out of bed, I head into the bathroom. While I wait for the water to heat, I brush my teeth and smile when I see imprints of Drey's hands and tits on the foggy glass...

...Drey was on the bed, breathlessly staring at me. After I feasted on her delicious cunt, I jerked myself off, covering her body with my cum. Never had a sight been more beautiful. "You look stunning with my cum all over you."

"And you look gorgeous with my arousal all over your chin."

"Guess I should clean you up so I can get you dirty again."

"I like that plan."

Surprising me, she army rolled off the bed and padded naked into the bathroom. By the time I entered the room, the shower cubicle was full of steam, with Drey inside. Her tits are pressed up against the glass. Her hands are above her head, and she's poking her ass out. "I think we should get dirty one more time," she purred. Who am I to deny a naked woman in the shower with her ass sticking out and begging to be fucked?

Reaching down, I stroked my cock and stepped into the shower. Standing behind her, she looked at me over her shoulder and waggled her eyebrows.

"Something you want?" I playfully asked, as I continued to stroke my dick.

"You," she panted.

Letting go of my dick, I rubbed her ass cheeks in my palms and squeezed. Then I pulled my hand back and slapped her ass. Her milky skin turned pink.

After I slapped her ass three times, she begged, "Please."

Taking her hips in my hands again, I slid my shaft down her crack and pushed in. She moaned and the sound was music to my ears. Pressing my front to her back, I pushed her into the glass, hoping it would hold, as I began to fuck her—hard.

She turned her head to look directly into my eyes. "Kiss me," she demanded.

Leaning forward, I covered her mouth with mine, and I kissed her deeply.

Pulling out of her, I spun her around, and before she could protest, I lifted her up. She wrapped her legs around my hips, and I impaled her on my dick. Pressing her back into the tiled wall, I kissed and fucked her like my life depended on it.

As the memory fades, I grunt and spray my seed all over the shower wall, giving myself another memory.

Stepping under the rainwater head, I wash myself, and once I'm clean, I step out. Drying myself, I change into my clothes and pack my bag. Drey and I are on the same flight home. Again, I upgraded her ticket and, like the trip out, what do you know, she's my seatmate.

Exiting my room, I wheel my suitcase behind me, and while I wait for the elevator, I'm joined by Drey. "Ms. McKeown," I say in greeting.

"Bastian," is all I get in return, but at least she didn't ignore me.

"Are we going to finish our conversation?"

"Nope," she defiantly states. "There is nothing to finish. You and I are nothing but colleagues."

"Who have seen each other's 'O' faces."

"That's moot."

Before I can press her further, the elevator arrives. "After you," I offer, placing my hand against the doorframe, allowing her to step in before me.

"Thank you," she utters as she walks past, and I get a whiff of her scent. I've never really smelled a woman before, but then again, I've never felt the things I feel for Drey with anyone else either.

"You coming?" The sound of her voice snaps me back to the present. With a nod, I step in, wheeling my case behind me. Reaching over, I press the button for the lobby. Silence envelops us. It's not awkward, but it's also not pleasant either.

"I guess you've arranged my ride to the airport?"

"I have."

"Well, it'd be silly to head to the same place separately."

"And I presume that you're also on the same flight, and by some miracle, you're my seatmate?"

"It is a small world."

"Mmmhmpf," she replies. I have to hold back my smile at the frustration billowing out of her. I think I've found a new hobby—taunting Audrey McKeown.

The trip to the airport is uneventful, and I behave, even if it was hard to hold back. We've passed through security, and Audrey excuses herself to use the restroom, but I think she just wants to get away from me. My suspicion is confirmed when I see her exit. She looks around for me, and when her gaze lands on mine, she quickly averts it and heads to the opposite side of the lounge.

I'm just about to head over to her when an

announcement comes over the speakers, informing us of a flight delay due to an engine issue. Excitement builds at the thought of staying another night in New York with Audrey. New York will always hold special memories of her. My cock likes said memories, but I tell him to behave as I make my way over to Audrey.

"Looks like we're delayed."

"Why do I feel like you had something to do with this?" she asks as I drop into the seat next to her.

"You got me, I fidgeted with the left phalange while you were in the bathroom just now."

"Did you just quote *Friends*?"

"I did, yes."

"Really? You like *Friends*?" she incredulously asks.

"If you must know, I love that show. Phoebe is my favorite character, and I think Rachel should have ended up with Joey."

"I approve of *Friends*, but you're wrong on the Rachel/Joey front. Ross was always her endgame."

"Agree to disagree," I tell her.

"Fine," she harrumphs, "but for the record, you lost points with that."

"But I make up for it with what I can do with my tongue." I waggle my eyebrows at her, while at the same time an older lady beside me scoffs. Drey tries to school her smirk, but I see it. "Shall we get a drink while we wait?"

"I need to get some work done, my boss—"

"Is demanding you have a drink with him. Work can wait."

She stares at me, and I feel like she's going to protest again, but then her head starts to bob up and down. "Fine, but it's just a drink."

24

AUDREY

ONE DRINK TURNED INTO THREE, and by the time our flight is called, I'm a little tipsy.

Bastian, like he always does, surprises me and is a total gentleman. Not once does he flirt with me, and he doesn't say anything inappropriate. The more we talk, the more I start to see another side of him. It almost makes me wish things could be different with us, but at the end of the day, he's my boss and there's a company policy. Yes, I fucked—pun intended—up and slept with him again after starting at Blackstone but that man, he seems to know how to lower my inhibitions ... and my panties.

An unladylike snort slips out, and I can feel his gaze on me.

"Care to share the joke?"

Shaking my head, I purse my lips. "I'm good."

"Can I get you anything to drink?" the flight attendant asks once we're seated in first class—again. She's all googly eyed over Bastian, and for some reason, seeing that pisses me off. Women fawn over him all the time, and who can blame them? He really is an attractive man, and when you take away his cockiness, he's a great man, too.

"Whiskey, neat," he tells her, "and the lady will have a mimosa."

Smiling over at him, I notice the attendant scowl when she realizes that he's not paying her any attention. Inwardly I snarl. *Suck it, bitch.* Again, I chuckle.

"Going to share the joke now?"

"Nope." I shake my head. "I'm good."

Pulling out my laptop, I lift the screen up, but it's soon snapped back down. "Your boss said no work."

"But—"

"It can wait, Drey."

"I ... I, fine," I relent.

Putting my laptop away, I settle back into my seat. The attendant returns with our drinks, once again flirting with Bastian, and this time, I growl out loud. Both of them turn their attention to me, and my cheeks darken in embarrassment.

"You all right there, dear?" Bastian questions, smirking like the bastard he is.

"Fine, just clearing my throat."

"A toast," he proposes, lifting his glass in my direction.

"What are we toasting to?"

"To you, the best editor Blackstone Publishing has ever had."

"You haven't seen my work yet."

"Audrey, just take the compliment."

"Fine," I relent. "Thank you."

He leans closer to me, and like a moth to a flame, I lean into him. "We could always toast to what we did last night, because that definitely needs to be celebrated."

"Just when I think you're not a pig, you go and say something like that."

"You say pig, I say charming, sexy, and vivacious."

"Oh my God, you really are conceited."

"Why thank you," he cheekily replies.

"It wasn't a compliment, and just so you know, I will never sleep with you again."

"We'll see about that. I always get what I want, Audrey, and I want you. Again, again, and again. Finding you in my bed is my new hobby."

"Well, you'll forever be searching, because that will never happen again."

"Never say never, Audrey."

"Never," I defiantly state, but even as the word passes through my lips, I don't even believe me.

25

AUDREY

...SIX WEEKS later

"Ugh," I groan after throwing up—again. "This stomach flu can go to hell," I mumble as I flush and stand up. Flipping the faucet on, I rinse my mouth and shuffle back to bed. Snuggling under the covers, I realize I need to let work know I'll be out again. Reaching over, I grab my phone and text Lainey.

AUDREY

Still not feeling well, I'll be out again today

She replies almost instantly.

LAINEY - That's no good, rest up. Kerrie and Gav are out too

AUDREY

Fingers crossed you don't get it ... I'll try to look over that manuscript you sent me later

LAINEY

Nope, no work. Just get yourself better, the office is quiet without you

AUDREY

I need to work. I need the distraction to not think about my stomach

LAINEY

Fine but don't push yourself or you'll be out longer. Let me know if you need anything

A bullet, I think to myself. Death would be wonderful right now but I know I cannot ask my boss for that.

AUDREY

Thanks, Lainey

Dropping my phone beside me, I remember I'm supposed to have dinner with Rebecca and Nicole tonight, so I quickly shoot off a text to cancel.

AUDREY

I'm not feeling well, can we take a rain check?

Rebecca immediately replies.

REBECCA

You poor thing, need anything?

AUDREY

A bullet

REBECCA

That I will not do, I don't look good in orange ... plus they don't have the good chocolate in prison

NICOLE

Still?

Do you need anything?

Maybe you're pregnant?

Then I start to think about the sex I did have, but thankfully, we used protection, so I know I'm not pregnant. Plus, there's others at the office who are sick too.

AUDREY

It's going through the office, plus you need to have sex for that to happen

NICOLE

What about that sexy boss of yours?

AUDREY

I can't hear you over the vomiting

REBECCA

Feel better Xo

NICOLE

Look after yourself ... call me if you need anything

AUDREY

Thanks. Chat soon, ladies

Placing my phone on my bedside table, I pull my duvet back up and I try to get some sleep, but no sooner do I close my eyes, and I need to vomit again. I make it to the toilet just in time, but there's nothing left in my stomach, so all I really do is dry heave.

Leaning against the vanity cupboard, I tilt my head back and start to cry. I hate being sick, and it's making me all emotional. Ripping off some toilet paper, I wipe my eyes, blow my nose, and throw the used paper into the toilet before I curl into a ball on the floor mat.

Closing my eyes, I lie here and the coolness from the tiles is soothing, and before I know it, I drift off to sleep.

There's an incessant buzzing, and I blink my eyes open and realize it's the buzzer to my apartment. Standing up, I stretch my body after sleeping on the floor and walk into the living area to answer the apartment phone, "Hello?"

"Ms. McKeown, it's Jeff from downstairs. I have Mr. Blackstone here to see you. I told him you said no visitors, but he's quite insistent."

"Bastian is here?"

"He is, shall I send him up?"

Nodding, I'm met with silence, and then I realize he can't see me. "Please send him up, the persistent ass will keep hounding you until I do, but please, no one else."

"Yes, ma'am."

We hang up and I walk to the door. Opening it, I crack it open. Then I turn around and shuffle over to the sofa. Dropping down onto it, I roll onto my side and close my eyes.

A few moments later, Bastian barges into my apartment, the door banging into the wall.

"What the hell?" I hiss as he closes it behind him and marches into my apartment.

He places a brown paper bag on my counter and turns to face me. "You look like death," he says in greeting.

"Just what a girl wants to hear when she feels, well, like death."

"Sorry," he says, dropping his voice. "Can I get you anything?"

"A new body."

"Your body is fine. You don't need a new one. How about some chicken soup?"

"I don't have any."

"You do. I stopped and got some on my way over. Why don't you go and take a shower, and I'll reheat this for you."

"You don't need to look after me. I can do it myself."

"I know you can, but the office isn't the same without you."

"You're full of shit."

"I see your sass is still intact."

"And I see you're still a bossy ass."

"You haven't seen bossy, now, shower. Go."

"I'm too tired to argue with you and, hopefully, the sooner I shower and eat, the sooner you will leave me alone."

He mumbles something incoherent as I hop up and shuffle into my bedroom. Stripping off my clothes, I climb into the shower. The hot water beating down on my back is refreshing, and I have to admit, I am starting to feel better.

Tilting my head back, I let the water wash over me. The sudden change in body temperature causes me to become woozy, and I begin to wobble. My vision begins to dot, and then I'm falling, it's lights out for me.

There's a disinfectant smell in the air. The sheet covering me is scratchy, and I feel like I'm lying on cement. Opening my eyes, I furrow my brow when I realize I'm in a hospital room. There's a pressure on my hand, and when I look down, I see a large masculine hand covering mine. I drag my eyes up the arm, and my eyes widen when I realize it's Bastian sitting in the chair by my bed. His eyes are closed, and I take a moment to appreciate his fine form. As if he can sense me, he opens his eyes and smiles.

"Hey, you," he utters.

"Hi," I reply. "Umm, why am I in the hospital, and why is my head throbbing?"

"What do you remember?"

"I was in the shower, and then I woke up here."

"You passed out in the shower and hit your head on the way down. When I came in after hearing the bang, I found you naked and covered in blood."

Lifting my hand, I press it to the bandage on my forehead, wincing when I press too hard.

"You have four stitches, and they're keeping you overnight for observation because it's taken you a while to wake."

"Ohhh, umm, well, I guess, thanks for being there."

"You're awake, Ms. McKeown," a rather dashing doctor with an Irish accent says, walking into my room. "I'm Dr. Flynn Kelly, and I treated you when you arrived."

"Thank you, Dr. Kelly," I tell him, patting down my hair, which no doubt looks like a bird's nest since it was wet.

"Do you mind if I ask you a few questions?"

"That's fine," I tell him.

From next to me, Bastian rises. "I'll go get you a coffee and something to eat."

"Thanks," I tell him.

He exits the room, leaving me alone with the doctor. "How you feeling?"

"A little better. Head's a bit sore but the nausea I was feeling earlier has settled."

"Happens in the first trimester, but I assure you, it will ease up soon."

"Excuse me," I hiss, "first trimester?"

"I ... ummm. I assumed you knew." I shake my head and stare at the doctor in shock. "We ran blood tests when you arrived, and they revealed you're pregnant."

Like the good doctor, I stammer, too. "I ... ummm, are you sure? Could it be a false positive?"

"When was your last period?"

"I have one of those implant contraception things. I ... I don't get one."

"Well then, there's only one way to confirm." I stare blankly at him. "We'll do an ultrasound."

Everything happens so quickly, and within minutes, the doctor leaves and returns with a portable ultrasound machine. "We'll try this way"—he points to the wand in his hand—"but if I can't see anything because it's too soon, we can do a vaginal ultrasound. It won't harm the baby, but it might be uncomfortable."

"Mmmhmpf," I nonchalantly answer him with a nod but, to be honest, I'm not really paying attention. I'm too shocked to think clearly right now. *I'm pregnant.*

"Okay, you ready?"

My head nods but inside I'm screaming, *No. No, no, fucking no.*

Dr. Kelly squirts some gel onto my belly and begins. I can't be pregnant, but if I am, ohh, God. It's … but my thoughts are interrupted when the most magical sound echoes in the room.

"What's that?" I ask. "It sounds like galloping horses."

"That's your baby's heartbeat."

"I really am pregnant?" I ask him.

He nods and smiles at me. It's a smile that, if I weren't already pregnant, would certainly get a girl pregnant. "I'd say you're about eight weeks along, and if you look at the monitor…" Turning my head to stare at the screen, my eyes widen when I see a baby. *My* baby. "That's your baby there," he says.

"Holy shit," I mumble. "It's a real baby."

Covering my mouth, I stare at the screen, but the door to my room flies open and a deep voice from the doorway booms, "You're pregnant?"

26

BASTIAN

WHEN I HEARD that crash as I was unpacking the chicken soup I brought, my heart stopped. I called out her name a few times. When I didn't get an answer, I walked into her room and again, my heart nearly stopped when I saw her slumped in the bottom of the shower. There was so much blood, and I had no idea where it was coming from.

Reaching in, I turned the water off and pulled out my phone to call 9-1-1. Somehow, I managed to relay what I needed and what I was seeing. The lady on the other end assured me an ambulance was on the way, and then I hung up and covered her naked body with a towel. I wanted to move her, but I was scared I'd hurt her more.

Once the paramedics arrived, it was chaos—but organized chaos. Before I knew what was happening, I was in the back of the ambulance with Drey, holding her hand, and we were on our way to the hospital. She was deathly white. Her head had a bandage wrapped around it, and she was still covered in specs of blood. That image will be seared into my brain forever.

When she finally opened her eyes again, it felt like I could breathe for the first time since finding her on the floor of the shower. I've been so worried about her and I'm thankful she received such good medical care.

Stepping out, I head down to the cafeteria and order her a coffee, just how she likes it, a cheese sandwich, and a chocolate bar—because everyone deserves chocolate when they're in the hospital.

On my way back up, I stop by the gift shop but there's nothing I like, so I make a mental note to order her some flowers once she's out of here and home again.

Heading back to her room, the door is closed but it's slightly cracked. Standing here, I'm unsure if I should go in or not since I can hear her and the doctor talking. Then it registers in my brain what they're saying, and before I can stop myself, I push the door open and growl, "You're pregnant?"

The door slams into the wall and bounces back into me. Kicking it with my foot, I stomp into the room, and my gaze flicks between Drey and the machine next to her bed. "Did you know?" I snap, my anger rising by the second. Is this why she keeps avoiding me? Or was this just some scheme to get pregnant by the billionaire CEO and trap me? "I asked you a question," I shout when she doesn't answer me.

She's lying there in the bed, shock on her face. "Bastian," she utters my name, "I ... I—"

"You what?"

"Mr. Blackstone," Dr. Kelly's tone is unnerving, especially with his thick Irish accent. "You need to calm down, or I'm going to have to ask you to leave."

"Calm down?" I hiss. "You want me to calm down when I find out she's pregnant." My gaze snaps over to Drey's. "Is it mine?"

"It ... it ... it's..." she stammers and nods.

"Are you sure it's mine?"

"What's that supposed to mean?" she asks, hurt all over her face at me questioning her.

"For all I know, you're sleeping with other men."

"I'm not," she whispers. "I ... I haven't been with anyone since I met you."

"Really? Why should I believe you?"

"Why should you not?" she throws back at me.

"I don't know you."

"But you know me enough to stick your dick in me." She crosses her arms and glares at me. "I'd like you to leave."

"I'll go, but don't even think about keeping my kid from me, if it truly is mine."

Without saying anything else to her, I exit her room. I'm only a few steps into the corridor when I hear her start to cry. The need to go back and make sure she's okay is strong, but I know I need to calm down before I talk to her again. Pulling my phone out, I shoot off a text to Beau.

BASTIAN

Meet me at Bin 501, I need a drink

Pocketing my phone, I exit the hospital and hail a cab since I rode here in the ambulance with Drey. I've just closed the door and told the driver to take me to Bin 501 when my phone pings in my pocket.

BEAU

I'll be there when I can

You good?

"Ha," I chortle. "Far fucking from it, Brother."

BASTIAN

I'll fill you in when I see you, but it's been one hell of a day

BEAU

Good or bad?

BASTIAN

BEAU

If you're using emojis it must be fucked

Don't do anything stupid

"Too late," I mumble.

BASTIAN

…

BEAU

Well, that's ominous, who died?

BASTIAN

No one, but it is life-changing

BEAU

Do you need an alibi?

BASTIAN

No … but I might need a lawyer

BEAU

Fuuuuuck, I'm on my way

Leaning back in my seat, I settle in for the ride.

Climbing out of the cab, I look up and see Beau walking down the street. "You look like shit," he says when he reaches me.

"Love you too, Brother."

"Wanna tell me what this is all about?"

"I need a drink first."

Without saying a word, he slaps me on the back, and we head inside. Branson is behind the bar, and when he sees us, he smiles. Then his eyes widen when he takes me in, and without saying anything, he places two tumblers on the counter and fills them both. He follows it up with two tequila shots.

"Is it that obvious I've had a day?"

"Yep," he and my brother reply in sync.

"Thanks," I mumble, then I pick up both shots and

throw them back, one after the other. Wincing from the tart liquor.

"Case in point," Beau says. "Now, what's up?"

Dropping my head, I stare at the bar top. As soon as I say this out loud, it'll be true. Well, actually, it was true as soon as I saw that screen in Audrey's hospital room. "Audrey's pregnant."

Neither of them speaks, and when I lift my head, I see shock on both their faces. "Awesome, thanks guys," I snarl. "Good chat."

Beau finally speaks, "It's just, wow, umm, how?"

"Well, son," Branson says. "The penis enters the vagina and—"

"Not fucking funny," I roar.

"Well, that IS how babies are made."

"I know that, but what if it's not mine?"

"Please tell me you did not say that to her?" Beau asks, and without me even uttering a word, he punches me in the arm. "Oh my fucking God, seriously?"

"I—" but he interrupts me.

"I'm guessing she's just as shocked, and from what you've told me about this chick, she's not the type of person to fuck around. So now she's shocked, hurt, and pregnant."

"I'm a dick, I know," I snarl at my brother. "How do I fix this?"

"Flowers always work," Branson suggests.

Shaking my head, I smile when I think back to what she did with the flowers I sent her. "Not with

Drey." And I tell them what she did with the flowers and chocolates in the beginning.

"Ohhh, I love this chick," Beau unhelpfully states.

"Don't let Suzanne hear you say that."

"She already loves her too. But right now, I wanna know what you're going to do to fix this mess you find yourself in?"

Shrugging my shoulders, I shake my head in defeat. "I don't know. I know I fucked up, and I know I need to fix it, but how?"

27

AUDREY

He left.

He walked out and didn't let me say anything.

He didn't let me defend myself.

He .

Just.

Fucking.

Left.

My eyes well with tears, and before I know it, I'm sobbing my little heart out. My belly is exposed, much like my heart, and on the screen beside me is a picture of our baby—well, my baby. Reaching out, I run my finger over the image and begin to cry harder.

"You okay?" Dr. Kelly asks me, lowering my gown to cover my stomach.

"Yes. No. I don't know." I shrug and wipe away the tears on my cheeks.

"I'm guessing that's the father?" I nod. "And I'm guessing you and he are not together?"

"It's … complicated."

"When is love not complicated?"

Letting out a sigh, I cover my belly and gently rub it back and forth. "It's me and you, Munchkin," I tell my stomach.

"You'll be fine," Dr. Kelly states.

"How do you know?"

"I'm a doctor, I know these things. Now, getting back to you and you're baby, everything looks good with the scan. You will need to find an OB, and I recommend you start taking some prenatal vitamins. We will remove the implant in your arm—"

"Fat lot of good it did," I huff.

"No contraception is foolproof, well, abstinence is, but how boring would life be without sex?"

"Dr. Kelly, that's umm, you shouldn't really say that, should you?"

He nonchalantly shrugs at me. "I'd still like to keep you overnight for observation, but all going well, I don't see why you can't go home tomorrow."

"Thanks, Doc. You're sure the baby is okay?"

He nods. "Everything looks good, Ms. McKeown." He walks over to the machine, tears something off, and hands it to me.

It's photos of Munchkin.

Once again, my eyes well with tears. "I'm so emotional," I tell him, wiping at my eyes.

"It's the extra hormones in your system. Your body is doing something pretty magical right now, and when you hold your baby for the first time, you will feel a love like never before."

"You sound like you're speaking from experience."

"I am. My wife recently gave birth to twin boys."

"Twins, ohh God, how do you cope?"

"Coffee, lots of coffee."

"I'd kill for a coffee," I tell him.

"I'll see what I can do for you. In the meantime, rest up and I'll be back to remove your implant."

Without another word, he exits my room, taking the ultrasound machine with him. Rolling to my side, I stare at the pics of Munchkin and sigh. This is not how I planned on having a baby. But now that I'm pregnant, I'm scared but also excited to meet my son or daughter.

It's as if discovering I was pregnant made all the sickness go away. I feel the best I have in weeks, and I can't wait to get home, and as if he's in my head, Dr. Kelly enters my room. "Ready to blow this joint?"

"Yes." I smile brightly. "You'd think hospitals would have comfy beds and nice sheets, you know, aiding in recovery, but I swear, the sheets are full of thistles and the mattresses are made of concrete."

"You should try the beds in the on-call rooms, they're even worse."

"Well, that just sucks."

"Yep, but what ya gonna do about it? Beds aside, I just need to sign your discharge papers and then you're free to go. Who's picking you up today?"

"I am," a deep voice rumbles from the doorway.

"Didn't think I'd see you back here," Dr. Kelly says to Bastian.

"I'm not going to leave the mother of my child alone."

"Ohhh, so today Munchkin IS your child," I snap.

"Munchkin?"

"The baby, that's what I've named him or her. It's so impersonal, and I don't know, Munchkin is kinda cute."

"I like it." He walks into my room and places my overnight bag on the end of my bed. "I stopped by your place and grabbed you a change of clothes."

"How did you get into my apartment?"

"Jeff let me in."

Nodding, I purse my lips and stare at my hands in my lap.

"I'll be back with your paperwork," Dr. Kelly says, breaking the silence. He turns and before he leaves, he scolds Bastian for the way he treated me yesterday. It's endearing to see a man who doesn't know me standing up for me, and it's funny to see Bastian quaking in his boots.

"I'm sorry," Bastian utters.

"Don't apologize to me, you need to grovel and make it up to Ms. McKeown. You weren't the only one to get shocking news yesterday, and on top of that, she had a head wound to contend with as well. If I were her, I'd kick you out, but I have a feeling she's nicer than I am." Without another word, he exits my room.

A silence envelops us again. "Do you want me to go?" Bastian hesitantly asks.

Looking up, I stare over at him and notice the dark circles under his eyes, and I see remorse reflecting back at me. Shaking my head, I start to tear up again, "I ... I don't want to do this alone, Bastian."

"And you won't," he vehemently declares, his tone is forceful but also endearing. He walks around the bed and sits on the edge. He takes my hand in his and squeezes. "I was an ass yesterday."

"A big ass," I confirm.

"Okay, yeah, I was a big ass yesterday. I was freaked out after you falling, and then I heard you were pregnant and, well, I panicked because I was scared."

"You think I wasn't scared? I woke up in the hospital with a head wound, and then I'm told I'm eight weeks pregnant. What sort of mom doesn't even know they're pregnant?"

"A lot of women don't realize they're pregnant. Actually, one in fourteen hundred and seventy-five pregnancies go unnoticed until twenty weeks gestation."

"How do you know that?"

"I stayed up last night researching. You need to start taking prenatal vitamins, and you also need to reduce your caffeine intake and stress levels."

"I think *you* were the cause of my stress over the last twenty-four hours."

"I know, and I feel terrible about that but, Drey, I want to be there for you and our baby. And ... and I want you."

"Bastian, just because I'm pregnant it does not mean we need to be in a relationship."

"But—"

"No," I interrupt him. "This doesn't change anything regarding us."

"Well, I want to be there for you and the baby."

"And you will, but we don't need to be in a relationship. Nothing has changed. Well, things will change because, I guess, I ummm ... I need to resign,"

"Not happening," Bastian growls from beside me.

"But the policy—"

"Is going to be changed. It's a stupid, outdated policy anyway. Love is love."

"But we aren't in love."

"Semantics. You are not resigning. Your job will be safe."

"But—"

"Nope, no buts, and anyway, we aren't in a relationship, so technically no rule was broken."

"Pretty sure we broke that policy and then pissed all over the burning pages of said policy."

"That's quite an image, but it's moot. The policy is no more."

"And you can change it just like that?"

"I'm the CEO. I can do whatever the fuck I want."

"You're so cocky."

"You love it."

Yeah, I kinda do. "No, I don't. Now, get out so I can change. I'm ready to go home."

"It's not like I haven't seen you naked before."

"And you will never see me naked again, now, out."

Surprising me, he exits my room and closes the door behind him. Climbing out of bed, I open the bag he brought, and I smile when I see sweats and my oversized Crushers hoodie. Slipping off the scratching hospital gown, I change into my clothes, and just as I sit back down, there's a knock on my door. It's Dr. Kelly, returning with my discharge papers.

"I'm free," I singsong.

"Yes, you are. And don't forget to get those vitamins."

"Already on it," Bastian says from behind him. "While you were getting changed, I called in an order to the pharmacy. We can pick them up on the way back to my place."

"I think you mean my place," I tell him.

"No, mine. I don't want you alone."

"Bastian, that's not your call. I want to go home to *my* home."

"And you will be, but to my home."

"Not happening."

"I'll leave you two to it," Dr. Kelly says. He adds a quick, "All the best" and then he quickly exits my room.

"This isn't helping my stress levels," I throw at Bastian. "I want my bed and my things."

"Fine, I'll stay with you then."

"Oh my fucking God. You are—"

"Incredible? Amazing? Thoughtful."

"I was going to go with insufferable but I think egotistical also works."

"Thanks, babe—"

"Wasn't a compliment," I interrupt but the asshole that he is, ignores me.

"Now, get your shoes on. Then we can pick up your vitamins and get you home. And maybe some food too. You're hangry."

"I'll show you hangry," I snap, but like a good girl, I follow his instructions and before long, we are on our way, out to his car.

We stop at the pharmacy, and he races in and gets my vitamins. Then we stop at an Italian place, it's kind of out of the way but Bastian assures me it's worth it. And I have to agree, the lasagna I ordered is the best lasagna I've ever eaten.

After eating, we make our way to my place when

Bastian gets a call and has to leave. I say a silent thank you to the man above because it will give me some peace and quiet. The air has been tense since we left the hospital. Bastian and I still have lots to discuss, but I don't have the mental capacity to deal with that at the moment. So much has happened in the last twenty-four hours, and my head is spinning. That could be from my head injury, but whatever, I just want my bed.

After seeing Bastian out, I climb into my bed and blissfully drift off to sleep.

28

BASTIAN

Walking into Kerrie's office, I kick the door closed and look at my head of HR. "Did you get it sorted?"

She looks up at me with raised eyebrows. Then she leans forward, rests her elbows on her desk, and steeples her fingers. I immediately know I'm about to get a tongue-lashing. "Hi, Bas, nice to see you too. I'm well, thanks for asking."

Letting out a huff, I smile charmingly over at her. "Hello, Kerrie. You are looking well, how's your day been so far?"

"It's been great, even if my pushy boss demanded I drop everything to overhaul some policies that do not need to be amended." Her sass is on point today, but then again, it's on point most days.

"They do and did you get it done?"

"I wouldn't have called you if it wasn't done, but why are we amending the fraternization policy?"

"No reason." I shrug, dropping into the chair across from her, but my reply earns me another eyebrow raise.

"Don't bullshit me, who are you fucking? And do I need to get our lawyers on speed dial?"

"No one now, and no, we don't."

"What do you mean by *now*?"

Leaning back in the chair, I get ready for story time, and I begin to tell Kerrie everything in regard to Audrey, me ... and the baby.

"Well, I didn't see that coming."

"You and me both, Kerrie, but am I an asshole for changing everything in my favor? I mean, I fired Chad for doing just this."

"Occasionally you can be an asshole, but Chad was a class-A asshole, and most people here only tolerated him because of his position above them, therefore, this is nothing like that."

"Was he really that bad?"

She nods. "He was the worst of the worst, but you want to know why I know people will be okay with this?"

Now it's my turn to nod. "Everyone here loves Audrey," Kerrie states matter-of-factly, "But, Bas, at the end of the day, this is your company. You can do what you want."

"Is it not a double standard?"

"Not at all. Chad was an ass. This place is better off without him. So, what if you change the policy to suit you, perks of being the CEO," Kerrie says like it's that simple.

"Is it really that easy?"

She nods. "It is. This new policy still has rules, and I hope you don't mind, but I added that you cannot sleep with a direct line manager. However, if something does start up, they are to come and speak to us straightaway. We can decide on a case-by-case basis what we do, but there's always a way to make these kinds of things work, *if* you are upfront and honest. Secrets and lies will not be tolerated."

"Are you sure that's all it will take? And are you sure everyone will be okay with Audrey and me?"

"Yes and yes, but tough shit if they aren't. The two of you are about to have a baby together. That's a little more serious than just screwing, but as I said earlier, it's your company, you can do what you want." Nodding in agreement, I feel a little more at ease now. "So, you really knocked her up, huh? How do you feel about that?"

"I didn't handle it well at first—"

"What did you do?" Letting out a sigh, I tell her about what I said and did when I heard the unexpected news. "But Beau knocked some sense into me, and that's when I came up with the amendment plan. With that out of the way, now I can focus on winning her over."

"Are you telling me that the infamous Bastian Blackstone is having trouble wooing a woman?"

"Don't make me fire you," I snap. "Even though you're a pain in my ass, I kind of like you."

"You say the nicest things to me, Bas, but you and I both know, you have the wrong parts, and I'm happily married." Kerrie and her wife, Andrea, are disgustingly in love. They have a relationship I aspire to. "And since you shared with me, I'll share with you, too. Andrea and I are also having a baby."

"You were approved by the adoption agency?"

She nods, grinning brightly. "Got the call this morning."

"I'm so happy for you both. When does the lil slugger arrive?"

"Mom is seven months pregnant, so as soon as she gives birth, we'll be moms."

"Look at both of us, becoming parents."

"Fate works in mysterious ways," she tells me.

A chuckle escapes me, because she's right. Never in my wildest dreams did I imagine Drey and I would be having a baby together. All I wanted was to have more with her, and I guess a baby is more, but it's not the more I was expecting.

Now that this policy has been amended, her job is safe. All I have to do now is win her over, because by the time this baby is born, she will be mine and we will be a proper family.

29

AUDREY

...two months later

"Who the fuck is Dawn?" I mutter to myself as I read over the email on my screen that starts with *Hi, Dawn.*

Scrolling down to my original email, my eyes widen when I realize I sent the initial one with *Regards, Dawn.*

In all my thirty years, I've never ended an email with Dawn. Sure, I've done Drey and Dred, even Drew, but Dawn? *What the fuck, Drey?* I guess baby brain is a real thing. I'm so glad this was just an inquiry to a company about their cribs and not an official Blackstone Publishing email.

According to water cooler gossip from those who were close with Mara and Chad, I only got the job because I got down on my knees for Bastian. Aside from the fact I never met Bastian until I already had the job. But it's kind of hard to refute their claims when A: I'm pregnant with his child and B: He changed the fraternization policy to now allow dating.

And I have to say, being the talk of the office is not fun, especially when it's not true, considering Bastian and I are not dating. Not for lack of trying on his part. He really seems invested, but there's a part of me wondering if it's only because I'm pregnant. If I wasn't carrying his child, would he care about me?

My phone rings, startling me. "Audrey McKeown," I say in greeting.

"Aude, it's Rhi at reception. Poppy Parsons is here to see you."

"Please show her to the conference room, and I'll be with her shortly."

"Will do."

Taking a deep breath, I recenter myself before I gather the manuscript and the mock-up of the cover and head off to meet Poppy.

"Poppy," I call out when I enter the conference room, "it's good to see you."

"Oh my God, you're pregnant?"

"Yep, I am." I smile at her, rubbing my now prominent bump. In the last week I've really popped, and you can tell I'm pregnant. Before, people would wonder if I'd just eaten a big meal or if I was bloated. "I'm just over four months."

"Well, congratulations." She races around the table to me and pulls me in for a hug. "Who's the daddy?"

"Umm, Bastian."

Her eyes widen. "Please tell me you and that spunky boss of yours are now a couple?" Shaking my head, I chuckle when I see the dejected look on her face. "Why the hell not?"

"It's complicated," I tell her.

"When isn't love complicated?" She throws back at me, and again, I chuckle because she has the most complicated love life ever. One partner is tricky enough, but when there's three of you, I can only imagine the complications that arise from time to time. "But just know, I'm rooting for the two of you to get your shit together because blind Freddy can see the spark between you two. And the way he looks at you, it's romance novel worthy."

"Of course you'd say that. You're a romance author."

"Just stating the truth, and another truth is, you're glowing. Pregnancy certainly agrees with you."

"Thank you but we're here to gush over you, not me." Taking a seat, I look over to her and I can't hide my smile. "Poppy, those rewrites you did, chef's kiss." I kiss my fingers and smile brightly at her. "I loved the story before, but now, I love, love, love it. This is going to become a bestseller."

"You think?"

"Definitely." I nod enthusiastically.

"Yay." She excitedly claps her hands. "Do we have dates yet?"

"None locked in specifically, but I really want it out before Munchkin arrives."

"That soon?"

"Mmmhmpf." I nod. "You want a sneak peek at the cover?"

"Yes, yes, yes," she squeals, clapping her hands again.

"Okay, so, those amendments sparked an idea, and when I ran it past the designer, he loved my idea, and well, I hope you love it too." Pulling out my iPad, I bring up the mock-up and hand it over to her. Her eyes widen, and a megawatt smile appears on her face.

"Audrey, it's perfect and exactly what I had in mind. It's scary how much you and I think alike."

"Scary but good."

"Totally good!" She beams.

We spend the next thirty minutes discussing the release. With tentative dates locked in, we say our goodbyes, and I head back to my office. I'm yawning when I walk in.

"Are you getting enough sleep?" a deep voice asks, and I squeal in fright.

"Shit, Bastian, I didn't see you there."

"Answer me, Drey, are you getting enough sleep? Do we need to reduce your hours?"

"Yes, I'm getting enough sleep and, no, I don't need reduced hours."

"Then why are you tired?"

"Because it's Friday and it's been a busy week. Aaaaaand I'm growing a human being."

"Are—"

"I'm fine," I snap, becoming irritated with him. "Now, what can I do for you?"

"I was hoping you'd let me take you to dinner?"

"I'm not going on a date with you."

"It's just dinner, Drey."

"Well, I do like dinner so, yes, I will have dinner with you."

"Excellent. I'll be back to collect you at five-thirty."

"I'll see you then."

Bastian leaves my office, and I flop down into my chair. I know I said this isn't a date, but I haven't been able to stop thinking about what Poppy said. Does he really look at me like she said? Or is it all in her head?

My concentration is shot, and I'm struggling to focus and stay on task. My mind is a jumpy mess, and my stomach is fluttering. I'm nervous for dinner tonight, because deep down, I know it's more than "just dinner."

"I swear each mouthful is better than the last mouthful." Bastian and I are dining in the Italian restaurant he took me too after we found out I was pregnant and like the first time, the lasagna is mouth-wateringly scrumptious.

"I can tell. I was about to ask if I should leave you and your lasagna alone. The sounds you're making are making my dick hard."

"Bastian," I hiss. "You can't say things like that to me."

"Well, don't moan and be all seductive." He stares intently at me across the table. "You really are beauti-ful, Drey."

"You're not too bad yourself, Bastian." Then I quickly add on, "But this isn't a date."

"My friends call me Bas."

"I like calling you Bastian."

"Wanna know a secret?" I nod. "I kinda love it too, but I really love it when you're screaming my name as you come all over my dick."

"Bastian," I screech, "you also can't say things like that."

"That's the second time you've said that tonight, but by now you should know, I always say what's on my mind." He picks up his glass of wine and takes a sip. I watch as he swallows and suddenly get the urge to kiss him. "What are you thinking?"

"N-n-n-nothing," I stutter.

"Liar."

"I'm not lying," I refute.

"I think you are, but I'll let it slide. Shall we get dessert?"

"I'm going to get fat if I eat another bite."

"You are far from fat."

"I am," I whine. "See?" Leaning back in my chair, I rub my belly and show him.

"You're pregnant, not fat. There's a difference."

"But if I keep eating like I'm eating, I will get fat." Lately, food is all I think about, and what's most shocking, I keep thinking of, and eating, a pickle sandwich on rye with pickle mayonnaise. It's the best tasting thing ever, it even trumps the delicious lasagna I just had.

"If anything, you're underweight for how far along you are. Did you know that now, at four months, Munchkin is the size of an avocado. Her ears and eyes have developed, and he or she can now hear. Studies show that we should talk to the baby. It will help the bonding process when Munchkin arrives."

"You amaze me," I tell him. "You know more about being pregnant than I do and what I should expect and when. Munchkin is lucky to have you as their dad."

"And Munchkin is lucky to have you as their mom."

We stare at one another across the table. The air thickens. We each begin to lean forward, but the moment is interrupted when the waitress arrives, asking if we want dessert. We both decline, and Bastian asks for the check.

He settles the check while I use the bathroom, and when I rejoin him, he escorts me to his car. He opens my door, but before I climb in, he slides his hand behind the back of my head and presses his lips to mine. My eyes close, and I give myself over to the kiss. The sound of a car horn pulls us apart, and just like that, the moment has passed.

He helps me into my seat and then walks around the hood, climbs in, and pulls out of the parking lot. The car ride back to my place is quiet and awkward. He pulls up in front of my building but neither of us moves.

Turning to face him, I break the silence, "Thank you for dinner. I had a nice night."

"Me too. We should, umm, do it again soon."

"I'd like that."

"Me too."

Silently we stare at one another and, like earlier, the air around us thickens. Again, we lean into one another and again we kiss. Our tongues slip and slide together, and it's perfect, but what does it mean?

Pulling back, I rest my forehead against his. "Good night, Bastian."

"Good night, Drey." Then he leans down to my belly. "Good night, Munchkin."

Without saying another word, I climb out and head inside. "Evening, Ms. McKeown," Jeff greets me with a smile when I reach the entrance.

"Evening, Jeff."

Walking across the lobby, I enter the elevator and press the button for my floor. Pressing my fingers to my lips, I smile and realize I'm starting to fall for Bastian—but am I falling or is it just pregnancy hormones? Everyone is telling me to give it a go with him, but I'm scared. I have too much to lose, and I'm already an unwed single mom.

Entering my apartment, I take a quick shower before bed. Lathering moisturizer on my bump and legs, I change into my boxers and cami set and climb into bed. Contentedly, I sigh. The housekeeper was here today, and I have new sheets, nothing beats climbing into bed with fresh sheets. Well, maybe fresh sheets with freshly shaved legs but for tonight, I'll just have to enjoy the fresh sheets.

Lying here, I stare at the ceiling and think about our kisses tonight. They were perfectly perfect. A tingle begins to thrum between my legs. I've been a little horny of late, and my vibrator has been getting a bit of a workout. Reaching into my bedside table drawer, I grab the device out and turn it on.

Rubbing the tip over my nipple, I break out in goosebumps and that tingle turns into a full-on throb. Moving my hand down lower, I slip under the waistband of my boxers and into my panties. The tip of the buzzing machine brushes over my clit, and I shudder. Slipping it between my folds, I slide it up and down my slit. With my other hand, I fondle my breasts, squeezing my nipples and pinching them. I wish someone was here to suck on them, but for now, I'll just have to use my imagination.

Moving lower, I push it in and moan at the intrusion. Pressing the button at the end, the buzzing increases, and before I know it, I'm moaning through my release.

With a smile on my face, I head back into the bathroom, clean the device, and wipe between my legs. Heading into the kitchen, I drink a glass of water and then head back to bed.

Snuggling under the duvet, I rest my hand protectively on my stomach. I still can't believe I'm pregnant, and I'm really surprised that Bastian wants to be a part of my and Munchkin's lives, any way he can. I know he wants more than I'm willing to offer right now. As I lie here, gently rubbing my stomach, I kinda wish he were here too, but he and I come from such different worlds. Can we work?

He's more than proven to me that he's committed, and it's really surprised me. He regularly replenishes my vitamins, and he hasn't missed one doctor's appointment. He's really going over and above, but is it just out of obligation because of the baby? Or does he really care?

30

———

BASTIAN

THE SOUND of my phone ringing wakes me, glancing at my bedside table clock, I see it's just after midnight. Patting around for my phone, I finally feel it, but it stops ringing before I can answer. It immediately starts to ring again, and I see Drey's smiling face on the screen. "Drey," I say when I answer, "is everything okay?"

"Bastian," she cries, her tone is heartbreaking, and I immediately sit up, on edge and ready to go into battle. "I ... I need you."

"What's wrong?" I ask, climbing out of bed.

"I woke up and needed to pee but there's blood, Bastian. I'm ... I'm bleeding."

Holding the phone between my ear and shoulder, I pull on my jeans while trying to calm her down. "You need to take a deep breath. Hop back into bed, I'm on my way. Just hang tight, and I'll be there as soon as I can." One handedly, I pull my shirt over my head. I can hear shuffling through the line. "Where are you now?"

"I'm back in bed," she murmurs as I grab my shoes, tucking them under my arm.

"Good girl. Stay there and try to relax. I'll be there soon, baby. Do you want to stay on the line with me?"

"Yes," she whispers, and then she starts to cry. Her sobs cut me deep, and I hate I can't soothe her right now.

"Don't cry, baby," I tell her as I head down to the garage. "I'm almost in my car. I'll be there soon."

"Please hurry," she cries, and I hate hearing her so broken. After a brief silence she adds, "I'm scared, Bas."

Bas, she called me Bas.

"Try not to worry. I'm on the road now. I'll be there soon."

We're still connected, but we don't say anything. All I can hear are her soft whimpers, I hate feeling so helpless and so far away. I'm pretty sure I broke every traffic law, but after an eternity, I finally pull up in front of her building. I turn the engine off. "I'm here, baby," I tell her as I race up to the entrance. With closed fists, I bang on the glass door, garnering the attention of the night doorman. "Can I help you?"

"I need to get in. I need to get up to Drey ... she, she's bleeding and the baby and, I need to get in. Let me in," I growl, banging on the glass. The man hesitates. "Please," I beg, and finally he nods.

He lets me in, and I race to the elevators. I climb in as soon as the door opens. Pushing the button for her floor, I repeatedly press the *close door* button. "I'm in the elevator, Drey. I need you to hop up and open the door for me."

"Okay," she timidly replies.

"Good girl," I tell her.

A few moments later, the elevator arrives at her floor, and as soon as the doors start to open, I turn to the side and squeeze through. Entering the hallway, I run toward her door, and just as I arrive, it swings open.

"Bas," she cries when she sees me and throws herself at me.

Wrapping my arms around her, I rub her back and hold her tightly to me. "I'm here, baby." I kiss the side of her head. "Let's get you some shoes, and I'll take you to the ER to get checked out."

She absentmindedly nods, and I guide her back into her apartment. We head into her bedroom, and she grabs her shoes and slips them onto her feet. She looks up at me. "Bas, what if—"

"No," I interrupt, shaking my head. "We are not going to think negatively. Munchkin is going to be fine." She nods but I can tell she doesn't believe me. "Can you walk?" Again, she nods. "Okay, let's go."

Pulling her into my side, we exit her apartment and head back downstairs and out to my car. Buckling her in, I race around the hood, climb in, and pull away from the curb. Reaching over, I grab her hand and bring it to my lips, kissing her knuckles. Placing our joined hands on her thigh, I drive us to the hospital.

Pulling up at the emergency doors, I climb out, and when I get around to her side, I look into the car. Drey is just sitting there, blankly staring ahead, at least her tears have stopped.

Opening her door, I drop down to my haunches and reach into the car. Gripping her chin, I turn her head toward me. "Drey, babe, we're here and it's all going to be okay."

"How do you know?"

"Because I just do. Now, come on. Let's go get you and Munchkin checked out."

She nods but doesn't move. She just sits there—frozen—sadly staring at me. Her eyes are once again welling with tears.

"Drey, babe, what do you need me to do?"

"I ... I don't know."

Leaning into the car, I scoop her up in my arms and kick the door closed with my foot. She rests her head on my shoulder, and I walk into the hospital. Immediately, a nurse comes over.

"What's happened?"

"She's just over four months pregnant, and she's bleeding."

"Come with me," she says. She guides us to a cubicle, and now we're waiting to see a doctor. Drey is lying on the bed, the blanket pulled up to her neck, and I stand beside her, feeling helpless. I hate not being able to do anything.

After what feels like a million hours, when in actual fact, it was only ten minutes at the most, the curtain pulls aside and in walks Dr. Kelly.

"We meet again," he says with a smile. He looks to Drey on the bed and smiles at her. "I understand you've had some bleeding?" She nods. "Cramps?"

"Nothing out of the ordinary."

"How far along are you now?"

"Just over four months."

He nods. "Do you mind if I have a feel?"

"That's fine."

He walks over to the bed and pulls back the blanket. Her nipples are tight and poking through her cami, I want to cover her up, but I don't. I need to stand aside and let him do his thing. Reaching out, he lifts her cami up and presses around on her stomach. Drey just lies there and lets him press all over her stomach. "And everything is going well up until now?" She nods. "And what were you doing prior to the bleeding?"

Drey gasps, drops her gaze, and begins to fidget. *What was she doing?* "Ms. McKeown, what were you doing?"

"I, umm, before I went to sleep, *Iusedmyvibratorandhadanorgasm.*" Her words come out in a rushed mess, and judging by the tinge of pink on her cheeks, she's embarrassed.

"I see," Dr. Kelly says. "Well, since your blood

pressure is normal and everything feels fine, I think your earlier orgasm caused the bleeding."

"I did this to my baby?" she wails. "My pleasure caused this to happen? I'm so, so selfish. Oh my God." She looks up at me, tears welling in her eyes. "I'm so sorry, Bas, I ... I didn't mean for this to happen." She lowers her head and covers her face as she cries.

"Hey, it's okay," I tell her. Sitting on the edge of her bed, I take her hands in mine and squeeze. "Look at me, Drey." She shakes her head. "Drey," I growl. She lifts her tear-filled gaze to mine. "Drey, you did nothing wrong. The books say that changes to the cervix can occasionally cause bleeding, and an intense orgasm can sometimes do that. It's perfectly normal."

"Don't try and placate me, Bastian." *Great, we're back to Bastian.*

"Ms. McKeown, he's right. You did nothing wrong. This is one of those mysteries when it comes to pregnancy and the human body."

"But my pleasure caused me to bleed," she hisses.

"And walking upstairs can sometimes cause bleeding too," I tell her.

"What?" she screeches. "I ... I can't do this." She begins to cry again. "I don't want this responsibility anymore. Can you, can you do the rest?"

"If I could, I would. But Drey, if you ask me, you're doing a good job. The baby is good. You're good. Everything is good."

"But—"

"Nope, no buts. Everything is—"

"Good," we both utter at the same time. For the first time since we got here, she smiles and I know, it will all be, well, good.

"I'm going to leave now. Ms. McKeown, for peace of mind, schedule another appointment with your OB, but I assure you, you have nothing to worry about."

She nods and smiles at him. "Thank you, Dr. Kelly."

"It's my pleasure. I'll leave your discharge papers at the nurses' station. You can leave when you're ready."

Without another word, Dr. Kelly exits, leaving Drey and I alone again.

"Lose the smile, Bastian. I nearly lost our baby because I needed an orgasm."

"You did not lose the baby. And for your information, I'm smiling because I know how stunning you look when you come, and right now, I'm jealous of your vibrator."

"Trust you to go there."

"I'm a man, what do you expect?"

"I expect you to be angry at me for causing this."

"As Dr. Kelly said, there is no rhyme or reason to this. Next time you have an orgasm, nothing will happen."

"I'm never having an orgasm again. I will not put Munchkin at risk."

"You're going to go the next five months without an orgasm?" She nods, and I can't help but laugh.

"Why are you laughing?"

"Because you will not last."

"Wanna make a bet?"

"I can't, in good conscience, take money from a pregnant lady. But just know, next time you want a release, call me. I will make it so good that you and Munchkin will be floating in orgasmic bliss. Now, what do you say we get out of here?"

"I'd like that but, ummm, my home or your home?"

"Wherever you are is home. One of these days, that will be under the same roof, but for now, we will go to which ever home you want."

"I only have one home, Bastian, and that's in your arms. Can ... can I stay with you? Please? I don't want to be alone right now."

"Anything for you and Munchkin. Anything."

31

AUDREY

For the next two days, Bastian dotes on me hand and foot. I can't move without him wanting to know what he can do or if I'm okay. It's sweet but also suffocating, and it's clouding my judgment when it comes to this man. If anything, the last few days have confirmed what I've been trying to deny. I do want more with Bastian, but I'm scared to give in to my feelings because I don't want him to think I only want him to feel safe, or to satisfy my itch.

Multiple times now, he's said he'd do anything for me, but I'm not sure I feel confident asking him for what I really want, especially when I know he wants more. And I definitely can't ask him for sex, because the last time I had an orgasm, I started to bleed. I know Dr. Kelly said it'll be fine to do it again, but in the back of my mind, all I can think about is Munchkin's health and safety. Even if, right now, I'm hornier than a porn star.

My pregnancy hormones are in overdrive, and it doesn't help that Bastian is currently in the kitchen in gray sweatpants—yep, gray ones—and a black tee that highlights his muscular arms and hugs his chest. He's like a hero right out of a romance novel, and I'm a wanton hussy who wants him to ravish me on the kitchen counter.

"What's got you thinking hard, pretty lady?" The sound of his voice snaps me away from Spicytown, and when I look up, he's standing by the sofa staring at me and looking absolutely edible.

"Huh?" I ask, because his words didn't register.

"I asked you what you're thinking so hard about."

"Ohh, ummm, n-n-n-nothing," I stammer. He eyes me, knowing I'm full of shit.

He drops down onto the sofa next to me and places his hand on my thigh. His touch jolts straight between my thighs, and I almost moan out loud—see I'm a wanton whore. "You can tell me anything, Drey."

"Fine, I ummm, shit, how do I say this..."

"I find words generally work, but you could also draw your thoughts."

"I can't draw to save my life, but umm, right, words. Okay." I nod. "Well, you see, umm, I like you—"

"I like you, too," he reaffirms, and follows it up with a smile that, like his touch, zaps straight to my vagina.

Now my clit is pulsating, and I'm finding it hard to find the words I need.

"Shut up and let me finish," I hiss. He raises his hands in surrender, and I miss his touch. Reaching up, I grab his hand and lace our fingers together. Resting them on my thigh, my thumb runs over the back of his hand. "Okay, so, umm, the last few days have been terrible, but at the same time, they've been the best. You've gone over and above to make sure Munchkin and I are healthy and safe an—"

"And I always will."

"I know that and I, umm, I think I want more with you." I lower my voice on the last few words.

"What do you mean by more?"

"I ... I want us to give this thing between us a go. I want Munchkin to have parents who are together. Who—" But before I can finish my sentence, Bastian has my cheeks in his hands and he's kissing me. His lips meld to mine, and our tongues dance an erotic tango in and around each other's mouths. He slides his hands around to the back of my neck, and he gently squeezes, causing me to moan into his mouth.

"I love when you make that sound," he mumbles against my lips and then continues to make love to my mouth.

Lowering his hands, he slips them under my ass and lifts me onto his lap so I'm straddling him. Draping my arms over his shoulders, I pull myself into his chest. Our bodies become one, and everything around me fades into the background. His apartment could be on fire, and I'd be none the wiser. All I can focus on is Bastian and his tongue ... and his dick that's currently pressing into my folds.

Swiveling my hips, I begin to dry hump him. My heart is racing, my pussy is trembling, and my mind— it's clear for the first time in months. I want this. I want him.

"I want you," I murmur.

"You have me," he replies, and those three words cause the switch to flip. Sliding off his lap, I kneel before him. With my eyes locked on his, I reach into his sweats and pull his dick out. The tip is already glistening with precum. Licking my lips, I lean forward and swallow his shaft. He groans, and the sound vibrates over my body. Sucking him in deeper, the tip slides into my throat, and I moan around it. I bob my head, lapping at his dick like it's a melting popsicle on a hot summer day.

Sliding his hands into my hair, I lift my gaze to his and, with our eyes locked, he guides my head back and forth until he comes down my throat. He scrunches his hand in my hair, tearing at the follicles as he climaxes. Once I've licked him clean, I sit back on my haunches and smile up at him. "So, I ummm, guess that seals the deal and we're now officially dating."

"Feel free to reconfirm our dating status anytime with a blow job."

"I'll keep that in mind, now, I'm going to take a shower. Think you can help me wash my back?"

"As your boyfriend, I'm obliged to assist you in any way I can. It might be tough to see you naked and wet, but I take my boyfriend duties very seriously, so I will happily wash your back. And if you play your cards right, I might even clean your vagina with my tongue and fingers."

"Well, if you insist. I mean, good hygiene makes way for a healthy pregnancy."

"Exactly," he states matter-of-factly. He gives me a smile that has my vagina thrumming. Standing up, he offers me his hand. Placing my hand in his, he pulls me up to my feet but neither of us moves. We just stand here and stare at one another. A silence envelops us, but it's not awkward, it's perfect, and I realize, I'm happier than I've been in a very long time.

My happiness increases during my shower because Bastian does exactly as he promised—he cleans my vagina with his tongue, twice. Then we fall into bed wrapped in each other's arms. I blissfully drift off to sleep with his hand protectively resting on my belly.

32

BASTIAN

IF I THOUGHT WAKING up naked with Audrey in my arms was great, waking up with her mouth wrapped around my dick trumps that, and it's now my favorite way to wake up.

"Good morning to you too," I greet her.

She lifts her eyes to mine, winks, and gets back to the task at hand. She sucks my cock like her life depends on it, and sooner than is appropriate for a man my age, I come down her throat. She swallows every last drop, licks her lips, and looks seductively up at me from between my legs. "Morning, boyfriend."

"Morning, girlfriend and mother of my child. Can I just say, that is the best way to wake up, and I wouldn't be upset if you did that every day."

"Duly noted and, for the record, I think I would like to wake up one day like that too."

"Duly noted, now, go get showered. I'm taking you out for brunch."

"Will you be joining me?" She waggles her eyebrows and, as tempting as it sounds, I know if I join her, we won't be leaving this house until the middle of the afternoon.

"Rain check, baby."

She nods, climbs out of bed, and skips into the en suite while I lie here and admire her body. She's always had a smoking-hot figure, but with her rounded stomach and full tits, she's even more beautiful.

"I can feel you looking at me."

"I'm allowed to admire my girlfriend."

"Even when I'm fat?"

Jumping out of bed, I pull her into my arms. "You are not fat. You're pregnant and glowing."

"You have to say that."

"I don't have to say shit, and just to prove how much I love your delectable body, get on the bed and let me worship you from head to toe."

"What about brunch?"

"We'll do lunch instead. Now, get on the bed. I have a body to devour."

Audrey and I missed brunch *and* lunch, and now we're having a late afternoon meal, but I wouldn't change a thing. I did exactly as I promised— I worshiped her body from head to toe. I can't even blame her pregnancy hormones. This morning was all me. Hearing her doubt her body did something to me, and I needed to show her exactly how I feel about her.

"You're smiling brightly, Mr. Blackstone," she says, interrupting my thoughts of this morning ... and last night.

"I have lots to smile about." At my words, her lips lift into the brightest smile I've ever seen. "Looks like someone else is happy too."

"Ecstatically happy," she beams, but the moment is broken when a shadow appears over our table. Looking up, I see Chad Hastings hovering above our table, a look of pure hatred in his gaze, reminding me of when we ran into him in New York.

"Well, well, well, what the fuck do we have here? Looks like you are fucking after all." His gaze drops to Audrey's chest and stomach. Seeing him leering at her riles me up.

"Chad," I sneer his name in lieu of a hello.

"Don't fucking 'Chad' me you piece of shit." The sound of his voice garners the attention of those sitting around us. "You're such a hypocrite. You knock up your employee and yet, somehow, you both still have jobs. I was right, you know, assholes like you think they're above everyone else, but let me tell you, you're no better than me."

"Not that I need to explain myself to you, but Audrey and I were already acquainted before she started at Blackstone Publishing, and it wasn't unti—"

"I don't give a fuck, Blackstone. You're fucking a fellow employee, per the nonfraternization clause, you both should be fired."

"Since you left, things have changed."

"Of-fucking-course they have." He throws his arms up. "Fucking typical, I'm guessing you rewrote the rules to suit you and your piece of ass." He shakes his head and the look on his face turns evil. "You're fucking pathetic. I can't wait for the day it all falls down around you."

"Is that a threat, Chad?"

"Take it however you want, but I look forward to the day the almighty Bastian Blackstone gets taken down a peg or three."

Before I can say anything else, he storms away from Audrey and me, shoving a waitress on his way out. Jumping up, I help the waitress, and when I turn back to the table, I see that Audrey has paled.

"Fuck," I hiss. Returning to the table, I go around to her side and squat down. "Are you okay?"

"I ... I'm fine but, Bastian, do ... do I, well, you, need to be worried?"

I shake my head. "No." Reaching out, I take her

hand in mine and squeeze, hoping it will ease her worry. "That policy has been amended." She opens her mouth, but I press my finger to her lips. "That policy has been amended—"

"Right. In *your* favor."

Nodding, I stare at the mother of my child, but I unequivocally know I made the right choice in changing the policy. "Yes, it is in my favor, but I realized that love is love, and a job shouldn't stop anyone from following their heart. But he's right. I *am* a hypocrite. It was *me* who pursued you, but *you* abided by the policy." Once again, a smile graces her face and I know that, no matter what, we'll be fine. "Yes, it took some persuasion for you to see my point and finally come around, but when I want something, I go after it. And Audrey McKeown, I want you with every fiber of my being, and that applies both professionally and personally." A deep chuckle escapes me. "In case you didn't know, I'm quite fond of you, Ms. McKeown. Finding you was the best thing to ever happen to me." Without thinking, I blurt out, "I love you, Audrey."

"You love me?"

Nodding, I reach over and take her hand in mine. "With all my heart, baby." And I mean it. I've worked hard for everything I have, but it's time that I got to do something for me. Being with Audrey is the most fun I've ever had. She doesn't care about my bank balance. She doesn't care that I own a successful company. She cares about me, Bastian Blackstone the person, and that's why I love her.

My happiness increases when she reaches up to cup my cheek and utters, "Bastian, I love you too."

33

AUDREY

...four months later

THIS WEEK HAS FLOWN BY, and I'm glad it's nearly the weekend. We've just finished our monthly meeting, and I'm waddling back to my office. I'm almost eight months pregnant now, and I'm the size of a whale. Well, it feels like I'm that big. I can no longer see my toes, and if I think of any food, I have to have it or I become hangry, and I can inhale a pickle sandwich on rye with pickle mayonnaise at any time of the day or night.

Even though I'm uncomfortable and overly emotional, I wouldn't change a thing. I love being pregnant, and sex with Bastian is mind-blowing. Positions are limited now due to my protruding belly, but the climaxes are out of this world. Thankfully, no more bleeding or unexpected hospital visits have popped up.

Bastian tells me that's because I'm "getting the real thing and nothing can compete with him and his amazing dick"—his exact words.

Apart from my one-time bleeding issue, everything is going well. My blood pressure is a little higher than my doctor would like but not so high that he's concerned, and since he's not concerned, I'm not. Bastian, on the other hand, has become a worrywart. His protectiveness of me and Munchkin is sweet but also overbearing.

Speaking of the overbearing ass, he's still pressuring me to move in with him. I know it's the logical next step, but there's still a part of me that wonders if he only wants me because I'm pregnant with his baby. I know he's not the type of person to do something because society expects it, but its lingering at the back of my mind, and I think it's the reason I keep putting him off.

Picking up the manuscript that was recently submitted, I begin to read. I get to a steamy scene, and I swear it's one of the hottest scenes I've ever read. I'm so horny right now. I really hope Bastian is free, because I cannot wait till tonight. I need a release, and I need it now.

Slipping off my panties, I drop them into my purse. Standing up, I straighten my skirt and exit my office. I waddle around to his, and without knocking, I walk in.

Closing the door behind me, I lean against the wood and stare over at the man who, in such a short amount of time, has become someone I can't imagine not being in my life.

"Everything okay, momma bear?"

"Mmmhmpf," I reply, biting my lip.

"You sure? I can hear you thinking from over here."

When I first came in here, all I wanted was a release, but suddenly I need to know why he's with me. "Why are you with me?"

"Why am I with you?" he repeats, and I nod my head. "Well, for starters, you're pregnant with my child." I deflate over that being the first thing he went with. "You have a brilliant mind. You know random facts, you're sexy as hell, and I can't fucking wait to ravish you tonight and show you just how much I want and need you."

His words heat my already heated blood. I need him even more than when I waddled in here. Reaching behind me, I flip the lock on his door and push off of it. Lifting my hands, I begin to undo the buttons on my white blouse as I walk across his office.

"What are you doing?"

"What does it look like I'm doing?"

"It looks like you're undoing the buttons on your shirt."

"Very astute, Mr. Blackstone." Standing above him, I stare down at him and lick my lips. His gaze watches my tongue move. "Stand up," I command.

He does as I ask and steps into my personal space. Sliding his hand around my skirt-clad ass, he squeezes, and I moan. Gripping his tie, I pull him to me and cover his mouth with mine. His tongue sweeps into mine, and he kisses me passionately. I may have instigated this, but Bastian quickly takes control. He walks me backward until my back hits the glass windows in his office.

"What is it with you and glass?"

Shrugging at him, I grab his tie, pull him to me, and whisper, "I seem to have lost my panties."

"What's gotten into you?" he asks as he runs his hand down my side and underneath my skirt. He bunches up the material around my waist, drops to his knees, and leans into me. He nuzzles my clit with his nose and inhales. "You smell divine, Drey. Are you soaked for me, baby?" Nodding, I bite my lip and stare down at him. "I'll be the judge of that." He drags the tip of his finger through my folds, and I moan at his touch. "You're soaked," he growls, and before I can answer him, he pushes his face between my thighs, and he attacks.

Sticking his tongue out, he licks up and down my slit. He sucks and nibbles my clit, and finally, he presses a finger into me.

"Yes," I hiss, grinding his face into me.

Gripping his head in my hands, I ride his face as he devours me. Covering my mouth to muffle my sounds, I moan through my release. My body shudders, and I soak his face as I come and come and come. I'm still coming down from my high when Bastian stands up, lifts my leg, hooks it around his thigh, and thrusts into me.

"Yes," I mewl, throwing my head back into the glass.

"Careful, baby," he voices.

"I'm okay," I pant. "Just don't stop."

"Never," he growls. He continues to thrust in and out of me. My body is already buzzing, and I'm ready to explode again. He covers my mouth with his, swallowing my cries as I orgasm for the second time.

He follows suit, and once he's emptied himself inside of me, he kisses me sweetly.

"Well, that was unexpected," he says.

"You can blame the manuscript I was reading."

"That good, huh?"

"The storyline no, but the sex scenes? Wowsers."

"Wowsers all right."

He pulls out and lowers my leg. I can feel his cum running down my thigh, and he smiles at the sight. "I love seeing you all disheveled, with your tits out and your pussy red and puffy, dripping with my cum."

"You have such a way with words."

"Thank you, now be quiet so I can admire you against the glass like this."

"Shut up," I throw at him as I waddle into his bathroom and clean myself up.

When I return, he's sitting back at his desk. He hands me a bottle of water. "Drink."

"So bossy."

"You love it when I'm bossy."

"Only in the bedroom ... or in the office against the windows."

"You're a minx."

"Why thank you." Leaning down, I press a quick kiss against his lips. "You can pick me up at five."

"It's a date."

Kissing him again quickly, I exit his office and head back to mine, but I can't concentrate. I keep thinking about what Bastian and I got up to just now. I've never been so brazen like that before, especially in the office. Bastian and I generally keep the PDA to a minimum at work, and we've never done that before, but oh my God, I might need to review our stand on office shenanigans because that was H-O-double T hot.

The rest of the afternoon drags by and, finally, Bastian and I are in his car, heading to his place for the weekend. Tipping my head against the headrest, I close my eyes and exhale deeply. I'm exhausted. Today was tiring, especially after what happened in his office. Staring out the window of the car, I rub my belly. Munchkin kicks wildly and I find myself smiling. "I'm so glad it's Friday. I just wanna hurkle-durkle all weekend long."

"What the hell is hurkle-durkle?" Bastian asks, his brows furled in confusion, and I've never seen him look so cute—damn pregnancy hormones.

"It's an old Scottish term that means to lounge in bed all day."

"Where the hell did you learn that?"

"My great grandma." I smile when I think about her, may she rest in peace. She was an eclectic old woman, and no one was safe around her and her walking stick.

He just nods at me. "Well, can I hurkle-durkle with you?"

"You can hurkle-durkle with me anytime you want."

And that's exactly what we do. We spend the whole weekend hurkle-durkling together. As sad as it is to admit, it was the best two days I've had in a very long time, but it all came to an end Sunday evening when Bastian had to fly to Colorado. He's still on the hunt for a second location for Blackstone Publishing, and he's headed there to look at a building. I personally think he's only there to watch the Dragons play. I was surprised when I learned he was a Dragons fan. With him being born and bred in Chicago, I would have thought he'd be a Chicago Crowns supporter, like Beau. His brother is as obsessed with the Crowns as Bastian is about the Dragons. Beau even has his own suite at the arena here. Actually, I'm surprised they haven't named the stadium after him.

If I weren't eight months pregnant, I would have liked to have gone with him, but the overattentive bastard is refusing to let me do anything that may cause my blood pressure to rise, even if most of the time it's because of him and his doting. Thankfully, he will still have sex with me. That's the only "exercise" I'm currently allowed to get in.

Speaking of sex, he was nearly late for his flight because I needed him one more time before he flew out.

Lying here in bed, I stare at the ceiling above, and I know what I want to do about our living arrangements. Just hanging out in his penthouse this weekend was perfect, and I keep imagining life here. Nesting has set in, and I really want to set my nest up here with him, so I've decided that, while he's in Colorado, I'm going to move my things in here—permanently.

34

———

BASTIAN

Yesterday was a bust but, thankfully, the Dragons won last night so it wasn't a total shit heap of a day. The building I looked at was nothing like it was online, and I'm pissed I wasted the trip.

It was late when I got back to the hotel. I tried to call Audrey several times before my flight this morning, but she never answered. She's probably sleeping since it's still early. If she were living with me, I could call reception to make sure she's okay. I keep asking her to officially move in. I mean, she spends most nights at my place, and it's a good thing because her sexual appetite has been crazy. Not that I'm complaining, per se, but my dick needs a rest. I don't think I've ever had this much sex in my life. Pregnancy agrees with Audrey, well, except for her slightly elevated blood pressure, but it's turned her into a nymphomaniac.

When I can, I make her rest, and I know sometimes

it comes across as overbearing, but I don't want anything to happen to her or Munchkin.

I'm sitting in the back of the town car heading into the office. I try Audrey again, but I get no answer. She should be at work by now, and I'm starting to get worried. I'm just about to try her again when my phone rings in my hand. I smile when I see Audrey's name on the screen. "Hey, hey, baby momma," I singsong when I answer.

"Bas, it's Lainey."

Sitting up straight, my heart begins to race. "Why are you calling me from Drey's phone?"

"There's, umm, bee—"

"Is Drey okay? The baby?" I shout into my phone, garnering the attention of the driver.

"She's in the hospital."

"What? Which one?"

Lainey tells me, and I give the driver a new destination. After what feels like a million hours, we arrive at the hospital. I dive out of the car and race into the hospital.

"I ... I need to see Audrey McKeown," I tell the lady at the desk.

"And you are?"

"Her husband," I tell her. I know they will only let family in, and it's not a complete lie. She and Munchkin *are* my family and, one day, she *will* be by wife.

"She's in room 307. That's on the third floor, go..."

Without letting her finish, I race away from the desk. "Thank you," I call out as I turn the corner and head toward the elevators to take me up to the third floor.

The wait for the elevator to arrive is excruciating. I consider taking the stairs but just as I think that, the doors open. Patiently—impatiently—I wait for everyone to exit, and then I dive in. Repeatedly, I press the number three button, willing the doors to close. Finally, they do, then we stop at both floors and the people entering take for-fucking-ever. After an eternity, we reach the third floor. Squeezing out the door when they begin to open, I race over to the nurses' desk. "Audrey," I huff out. "McKeown"—another huff—"is ... is she okay?"

"And you are?" the lady behind the desk asks, her tone pisses me off but I know I need to remain calm. Losing my shit right now won't help anyone.

"Her husband." She smiles at me, but it does nothing to ease my worries.

"I thought the man who was with her was her husband."

"I don't know what you're talking about, but I just need to know, is she okay?" Then I add, "Please, just tell me that she and my baby are okay."

When she sees the anguish on my face, her whole demeanor changes. "She's still unconscious. Everything seems okay with the baby. She was very lucky."

"Ohhh, thank fuck." I run my fingers through my

hair. Looking at her name badge, I look back at her. "When can I take her home, Hettie?"

"I can't tell you that. But I can tell you, she has a sprained ankle, a broken wrist, a fractured cheekbone, and multiple contusions. We won't know if she has a concussion, as your wife is still unconscious, and until she wakes up, we won't know the full extent of her injuries."

Covering my mouth, I shake my head. I should have been here. I shouldn't have been in Denver looking at office space. Audrey and Munchkin should be my first priority. "What happened?"

"From what I know, she was assaulted, and in the scuffle, she was hit by a car."

"Ohhh, Drey. Can ... can I see her?"

"Of course." She smiles at me. She stands up and walks around to me. "Come with me and I'll show you to her room."

"Thank you." Nodding, I follow her down the corridor. She's muttering something, but I'm not paying attention, I just keep thinking about Drey and Munchkin. I can't lose them. They are my everything.

Looking up, I see a man and three women sitting outside a room. I pause mid-step when the man looks up and our gazes meet. Stepping around the nurse, I walk up to him. "What the fuck are you doing here?" I hiss between clenched teeth as I stare at the asshole before me.

"Bas," he says, standing up to face me. "I—"

"I said, what the fuck are you doing here?"

"I was there—"

"You assaulted her?" I growl. I'm on him in seconds. I scrunch his shirt in my fist, and I forcefully slam him up against the wall. Pressing my arm across his neck, I get right up in his face. My blood is boiling right now. I knew Chad had an issue with me and what happened when he left Blackstone, but this? This is un-fucking-acceptable. Be a fucking man and confront me. Not a pregnant woman—not *my* pregnant woman. "Why would you do that to a pregnant woman? How could you stoop so fucking low?"

"I didn't assault her, you fuckwad."

"Then why the fuck are you here?" Turning my attention to the women, I realize it's Lainey, Rebecca, and Nicole. "Why is he here?" I growl at them. My anger is misguided, and I know I'm being a jackass, but my world has just imploded, and now this asshole is here and it's the last thing I need.

"Bas," Nicole goes to answer me just as a deep voice from behind pipes up.

"Sir, I need you to step away, or I will have to remove you from the premises."

Turning my head, I see a security guard standing there with Hettie. He's got at least fifty pounds on me, so I reluctantly let Chad go. Without uttering another word, I walk over to Drey's room, open the door, and step inside.

Leaning back against the closed door, my heart

drops when I look to the bed. If it weren't for the machines surrounding her, the cast on her arm, or the bruises marring her beautiful face, you'd think she were sleeping. She looks so tiny in the bed, except for her bulging belly. A smile appears when I see that, even unconscious, she's worried about Munchkin. Her hand rests on her belly, protecting our baby.

One minute I'm standing by the door and the next, I'm beside the bed. Leaning over, I press a kiss to her temple and whisper, "Please wake up, baby."

Dropping down into the chair, I pull it closer to the bed and take her hand in mine. Bringing it to my lips, I gently kiss the back of it. "I can't lose you, Drey, I just can't."

35

AUDREY

My body feels heavy, and it aches like it never has before. There's a pressure on my arm and hand, but the pressure is oddly comforting and soothing. Cracking my eyes open, I furrow my brow when I realize I'm in an unfamiliar room, and there's an odd smell in the air.

Closing my eyes again, I wrack my brain trying to remember what happened, but it's all fuzzy, and then, out of nowhere, it suddenly clicks. "I'm in the hospital?" I mumble, my voice squeaks, and I groan in pain. My throat burns, and when I try to swallow, nothing happens because my mouth is drier than the Sahara Desert.

"Audrey?" A voice I would recognize anywhere garners my attention, and when I look down, I see Bastian staring intently at me. Then I realize the pressure I felt was Bastian's head on my arm and his hand holding mine.

Smiling at him, I utter a small, "Water."

Bastian lets go of my hand and pours me a glass. Holding a straw to my lips, I swallow. The cool liquid is like heaven on my throat.

"Bastian, why am I here?"

"You're in the hospital. You were involved in a little accident, but everything is okay. Well, okay as it can be, but the main thing is, you and Munchkin are safe. That's all that matters."

"She's really okay?"

"He is, yes." My smile widens because whenever I call Munchkin a girl, Bastian refers to him as a boy and vice versa.

Rubbing my belly, Munchkin gives an almighty kick, letting me know she is indeed okay. "I'm glad you're okay, Munchkin," I say to my belly.

"Are YOU okay?" Bastian sits on the edge of my bed, taking my hand in his again. He lifts it up and presses a kiss to my knuckles.

"I think so," I tell him. "A little sore."

"That's to be expected. You have a sprained ankle, a broken wrist, a fractured cheekbone, and some cuts and bruises." He pauses. "Do you remember what happened?"

Thinking about it, I smile when I remember I was going to surprise Bastian by moving in while he was away, but then memories of what occurred slam into me, much like the car did. My eyes well with tears when I realize how lucky I was. "I was heading to my place to meet up with Nicole, Rebecca, and Lainey. The four of us were going to move my things into your place as a surprise—"

"You were moving in?"

"I AM moving in," I inform him. "I want us to be a family, Bastian."

"You've just made me the happiest man alive. Do you know that?"

"Well, you make me the happiest woman alive, so watch out world, we're going to be happy, happy when I blow this joint."

"Okay, so you were going to meet with the girls and Lainey, and?"

"I was around the corner from my place when this young punk tried to take my handbag. I wasn't going to let him have it, so I tried to fight him off, but he punched me in the face, and I stumbled. Then this guy appeared out of nowhere. He pushed me to the side when the kid went to hit me again. He was like a ninja. He flipped the guy to the ground and bent his arm back. I shuffled backward, trying to get away, and the next thing I knew, I was flying through the air. I tried to cushion my belly on the way down, and I managed to protect Munchkin, but my head cracked against the pavement, and it was lights out. The last thing I remember was Rebecca screeching my name." Absent-mindedly, I rub my belly. "Munchkin is okay, right?" I look up at Bastian, scared that he's not okay. "I didn't dream that you said that did I?"

"No, she's fine."

"You were both very lucky," a feminine voice says from the doorway. Peeking around Bastian, I see a lady in a white coat standing there. "Can I come in, Ms. McKeown?"

Nodding, I smile at her. "I'm Dr. Elena Cruz. I was one of the attending doctors when you were brought in. How are you feeling?"

"Okay, considering what I remember, but are you one million percent sure Munchkin is okay?"

"I promise," she affirms with a nod. "You have a tough one in there, but it seems mom is too. I hear you tried to fight off your attacker while eight months pregnant."

"I didn't want him to get my handbag."

"Babe, I'll buy you a million of the damn things. If there's a next time, just give it to them."

"No, that was a one-of-a-kind handmade bag that I got at a market! I love it."

"Women and their handbags."

"Says the man who has a billion cuff links."

"That's different," he defends his cuff link collection.

"Agree to disagree?"

"Agree." He leans in and kisses me. "I love you," he murmurs against my lips.

"I love you too," I tell him.

"You two are cute together. How long have you been married?"

"We aren't," I tell her. She scrunches her brows, and I turn to Bastian. "What did you do?"

"I may have told them all that you're my wife." My eyes widen. "They wouldn't let me in otherwise, so I told a white lie and, really, it's not a lie because one day, you will be my wife."

"Will I now?"

"Mmmhmpf. I got you to move in with me. Marriage is the next step."

"You are something else, Mr. Blackstone."

"Why thank you."

"Wasn't a compliment."

Shaking my head, I turn my attention back to the doctor. After more scans, she informs me that I need to stay in for a few days for observation as I'm on concussion watch. She leaves Bastian and me alone, but a few minutes later, Lainey, Rebecca, and Nicole pop in for a visit. We all chat, and I thank them again for looking after me.

After I yawn for the third time, Bas kicks the girls out. He climbs onto the bed next to me and, within seconds, I drift off to sleep, happy and safe in his arms.

36

BASTIAN

Two days later, Audrey is discharged, and I cannot wait to get her home. *Home.* I love saying that. Little does she know, while I've been here with her, I've had people move all her things into my penthouse. I also have a surprise in store for her, too. I really hope she loves what I've done, but if not, we can always redecorate. We still have time.

"Follow up with your doctor in six weeks about the wrist, but everything else looks good."

"So, I can go home?" Audrey asks Dr. Cruz.

"You sure can. I'll get the paperwork processed, and I'll leave it with Hettie for you to collect on your way out."

"Thank you so much for looking after Munchkin and me," Audrey says. With a nod, Dr. Cruz leaves. Audrey slips on her ballet flats and then looks to me. "I can't wait to sleep beside you tonight."

"Me too, baby, me too."

Pulling her up and into my arms, I hug her, then kiss her. I kiss her with everything I have. I'm so thankful for finding her. So thankful she and our baby are okay and over the moon that she's finally mine. Audrey McKeown is mine and I'm going to spend the rest of my life finding her. Looking after her. Loving her. She's it for me.

Game over.

Case closed.

The-fucking-end!

"I'm so sorry he hurt you," I tell her.

"You don't need to apologize, he's the one who did what he did but, Bastian, I'm fine. I promise. And so is Munchkin, he or she is a fighter."

"Just like his mom."

"Speaking of Mom, Mom is hungry. Mom really wants—"

"A pickle sandwich on rye with pickle mayonnaise."

"How did you know?"

"I think I know you pretty well, Ms. McKeown."

"Is that so, Mr. Blackstone?"

"That's a fact. Now, let's get you a pickle sandwich on rye with pickle mayonnaise, and then I'm taking you home."

"Speaking of home, when I was assaulted, I was going to my apartment to pack. I ... I wanted to move my things to your place as a surprise for when you arrived home."

"I know."

"And I still do. You know the other week, when I told you I only have one home and that's in your arms?" I nod. "Well, I want to be in your arms all the time."

"I know, so while we've been here, I've had people moving you into my place."

"Of course you did." She shakes her head and slides her arm around my waist. She looks at me and I see nothing but love radiating up at me. "So, what do you say, roomie, should we get out of here?"

"Hell-fucking-yes." Spinning her around, I cover her mouth with mine and I kiss her deeply. Pulling back, I rest my forehead against hers. "You have made me the happiest man alive, Audrey, and I'm going to spend every waking moment loving you."

"I like the sound of that, but can you love me while I'm eating my pickle sandwich?"

"Anything for you, baby, anything."

Audrey is pulling her jacket on when there's a knock at her door. We both look up and there's two police officers standing there. "Can we help you?" I ask them.

"Bastian Blackstone?"

"That's me."

"I'm Officer Kate Lane, and this is my partner, Ivy

Bonham. I'm going to need you to come down to the station for a chat."

"Can I ask what this is in regard to?"

"We need to discuss with you allegations that you assaulted Chad Hastings."

"The fuck?" I hiss. "He's seriously pressing charges?"

"He claims you assaulted him."

"I didn't hit him, but I did push him up against the wall, but it was all a misunderstanding."

"He says you punched him and accused him of the assault of Audrey McKeown."

"I—"

"Chad didn't assault me," Audrey interrupts me. "It was that kid when he tried to take my handbag. Chad, he ... he intervened, and when I was walking backward in shock, that's when I was hit by the car."

"Are you Audrey McKeown?" she asks Audrey.

"I am," she says, taking my hand and squeezing. The gesture immediately calms my inner beast.

"I'm going to need you to come in and give your statement regarding the incident."

"Is that really necessary?" I ask on her behalf. "She's just been discharged."

"It is. We need her version of events to finish the report."

"Well, can we at least get her a pickle sandwich on rye with pickle mayonnaise before we come in?"

"A what?" Both officers scrunch their faces up.

"Hey," Audrey growls, "don't knock it till you try it."

"I remember when Marco's wife was pregnant with twins, she loved ice-cream and hot sauce."

"Ohhh," Audrey coos, "that sounds delicious."

"You've created a monster," I tell the officer. "I promise that we'll both come down as soon as Audrey's cravings have been satisfied."

"That's fine, but if you don't show up today, I will issue a warrant for your arrest, Mr. Blackstone."

"That won't be necessary. We'll be there."

She gives me her card, and the officers leave. Audrey is laying into me before the door clicks shut. "You assaulted Chad? Why? What is wrong with you?"

"Calm down, Drey. It's not good for the baby."

"And neither is having my baby daddy locked up. Why would you assault him?"

"I didn't assault him." She eyes me. "Well, I may have manhandled him, but I did not assault him. When I saw him outside your room, I lost it. I wasn't thinking clearly. I was panicked about you and Munchkin, and when I saw him leaning against the wall, I just lost it."

"That's not like you at all."

"I wasn't thinking clearly."

"Ya think?" she snaps at me.

"Don't get sassy with me, woman."

"Well, don't act like a dick. Now, let's get me my sandwich. Then we will come up with a plan that doesn't involve you in orange, because even though you're a sexy billionaire who can rock anything, orange is not your color ... and I refuse to give birth while my baby daddy is in the clink."

"I am not going to jail, and, for your information, I can totally rock orange."

"Let's agree to disagree."

She takes my hand, and we exit the hospital.

Climbing into my car, I drive to the closest deli for her to get her gross sandwich, and together, we come up with a game plan to get me out of the trouble I find myself in.

37

AUDREY

Two long hours later, we leave the station, and Bastian is a free man—no orange jumpsuit for him. He wasn't charged, because during their investigation, they obtained statements from Lainey, Nicole, Bec, and the hospital staff who were there. All of them confirmed Bastian's story that he only pushed Chad up against the wall in anger, no fists were involved. While yes he shouldn't have done that, it didn't warrant an assault charge.

After another interview with Chad, he confessed he was trying to ruin Bastian for firing him. While yes, that company policy was outdated and stupid, to try and charge someone with assault because you're butthurt is such a douche thing to do. He really is a Chad.

Due to that, the investigation into Bastian was

dropped, no charges were brought against him since he didn't technically assault Chad. The officers did suggest that Bastian should stay away from him and that's something I'll happily help with. Munchkin and I need him. I will do everything I can to help him because that's what you do for the person you love. You help them, even when they do stupid things.

My attacker and the guy who hit me however, weren't as lucky. The guy who attacked me was charged with aggravated assault. The driver who hit me was charged with a DUI and reckless driving— turns out his blood alcohol level was one of the highest on record. He could hardly speak when the police arrived on the scene.

I'm so relieved that Bastian is free. I don't think I could handle it if he were taken away from me. "Promise me you will never do anything like that again," I tell him as we climb into his car to head home.

"As long as you promise never to do what you did again."

"Can't say I'm planning on getting assaulted or hit by a car again, especially while pregnant." I lift my cast-covered arm. "This is going to make life harder when Munchkin comes."

"I've got you, babe, I've always got you."

"And I'm the luckiest woman in the world."

"Well, in that case, I'm the luckiest man."

He leans across the center console and kisses me. It's toe-curling, and if I weren't the size of a whale right now, I'd climb over into his lap and have my wicked way with him, and that's *not* the pregnancy hormones talking. He breaks the kiss first and cups my cheek. Leaning into his palm, I feel safe, secure, and loved. Life could not get any more amazing ... or so I thought.

38

BASTIAN

On the drive back to the penthouse, I'm a bundle of nerves, and I don't get nervous. Ever. But this woman causes me to do many things that I've never done in the past, and the most amazing thing of all, falling in love. I never thought I'd find a woman who is my everything. My day starts and ends with thoughts of her.

Our trip home is delayed when Audrey demands that I stop at the deli around the corner from home so she can get another one of those disgusting sandwiches she loves so much. I will admit though, seeing her so happy while eating "the best sandwich ever" makes the grossness and delay worth it.

With her tummy full of pickles and rye, we're finally home. Pulling into the underground garage, I park in my spot and turn off the engine. Climbing out of the car, I race around to her side and help her out. Lacing our fingers together, I bring them to my lips and kiss her knuckles. She smiles at me in that adorable way that gives me the warm fuzzies. Pressing a kiss to her temple, we walk over to the elevator and climb in when it arrives.

The metal car whisks us upstairs, and when we arrive, I scoop her up into my arms and carry her over the threshold. Placing her down on her feet, her smile widens when she sees the flower arrangement on the entryway table. "Do you have shares in a florist?"

"No, but I should look into buying some." She laughs and it's music to my ears. She kicks off her ballet flats, walks over to the flowers, and runs her finger over one of the petals. Watching her so relaxed in our home is heartwarming, but then I think about the room down the hall and my nerves, once again, ramp up.

Needing to get it over with, I walk up behind her and slide my hands around her waist. Resting my palms on her belly, she leans back into me. "I have a surprise for you," I whisper into her ear.

She spins around in my arms and drapes hers over my shoulders. "Is it your penis?" She waggles her eyebrows at me, and I can't help but chuckle.

"It is not, but I'm sure we can arrange that. First, do you trust me?"

"With my life," she emphatically states.

"Okay, close your eyes and take my hand."

Without any hesitation, she steps back, holds out her hand to me, and closes her eyes.

Taking her hand, I cover her eyes with my other

one because I don't trust she's not going to peek. Guiding her through the living room, we turn into the hallway and head down to what used to be one of the guest rooms. Pushing open the door, I take a deep breath, remove my hand from her eyes, and whisper, "Open them."

Stepping to the side, I stare at her as she takes in the room. What used to be a spare bedroom with white walls, a queen bed, and a dresser is now a nursery right out of a baby magazine. The walls are now a buttery-yellow. There's a soft rug on the floor. On the far wall is a dark wooden crib, and next to that is a set of drawers with a changing table on top. Above that is a shelf with all the necessities for a diaper change. In the corner is a recliner, which I'm told is a game changer for middle of the night feeding. The wardrobe is waiting to be filled with baby clothes, but my favorite part of the room is the mural that wraps around the top of the walls. In one corner, a tree stretches up from the floor and around the ceiling line is a long branch. Hanging off the branch are different sized leaves with letters of the alphabet. I know Munchkin is too little to know the alphabet yet, but the books I've been reading about children and their development state that bright colors and words are great for their minds.

Audrey spins in a circle, taking it all in, but I can't read her expression. I begin to wonder if I've over-stepped, but when she faces me again, she's smiling. "Bastian, this ... this is everything a nursery should be and more. Never in my wildest dreams did I think Munchkin would have a room like this."

"So, I did good?"

"You did fantastic, Mr. Blackstone." She bites her lip. "How will I ever thank you?" She traces her fingertip down her neck and across her chest before dipping into her cleavage.

"How about you follow me into our bedroom? I'm sure we can come to some sort of arrangement."

"I love that plan," she huskily replies. "And for the record, you are going to be the best dad in the whole entire world. Munchkin and I are very lucky to have you. I love you, Bas."

"You have that wrong, Audrey. I'm the lucky one. Finding you three times pushed my luck, but you loving me and calling me Bas makes me the luckiest son of a bitch alive."

EPILOGUE
AUDREY

...four years later

"Oʜʜʜ Goᴅ," I moan as Bastian sinks into me from behind. Waking up with his dick sliding into me is one of the best ways to wake up.

"Shhhh, or you'll wake Noah."

"That kid could sleep through an F5 tornado."

"You wanna risk testing that theory?"

"No," I pant. "Just shut up and keep fucking me.

"Well, shut up and let me finish fucking you."

"So bossy," I tease, and my words turn into a pleasurable groan. Even after all these years, sex with Bastian is just as good as that first night. And it's even better when I'm pregnant. I'm currently fourteen weeks pregnant—with twins. I thought I was a horny bitch when I was pregnant with Noah, but with the twins, aka the *Twinkies*, I'm insatiable. I guess there's twice as many hormones in my system this time.

"I'll show you bossy." He pulls out of me and flips me onto my stomach. Gripping my hips, he lifts me up and slams back into me. I moan into the pillow and push myself up onto all fours. Doggy style makes each thrust of his dick deeper and deeper. Bastian slides his hand around to my clit and presses down on the sensitive bundle of nerves. "Baaaaaaaaaaaastiiian," I moan.

"Shhhh," he grunts, slapping my ass.

Another sound slips through my lips. It's inhuman sounding, but right now, all I can focus on is the pleasure building.

"Do I need to stuff your mouth with my cock to shut you up?"

"I ... I wouldn't mind that."

Before I know what's happening, I'm on my back, Bastian's straddling my chest, and his dick is right there. Licking my lips, I open my mouth to suck on his swollen cock that's coated in my juices. Then we hear the stomps of our little man racing down the hallway. "Shit," we both hiss at the same time. Bastian dives off of me and pulls the duvet up, covering our nakedness just in time. Seconds later, the door swings open, and Noah runs across to the bed and jumps up.

"Watch Mommy's tummy," Bastian warns, grabbing Noah and pulling him on top of him. Seeing Bastian as a father is just as sexy as I imagined. He's doting and attentive and the best person I could have asked for to be the father of my children.

"Good morning, baby," I tell him, ruffling his hair.

"Morning, Mommy. Are you having bacon and chocolate sauce bagels again this morning?" He scrunches his nose at this pregnancy's food craving.

"I will be, but I'm happy to make you and Daddy whatever you want."

"Chocolate pancakes?"

"Ohhh, chocolate pancakes with bacon sounds delicious."

"Eeewww, Mommy. That's gross."

"Did you know," Bastian says, "when you were in Mommy's tummy, she ate pickle sandwiches on rye with pickle mayonnaise."

"Eeewww, Mommy. That's grosser."

"I don't think grosser is a word, but why don't you go watch *Bluey* while I get started on your chocolate pancakes?"

"Yes." He pumps his little fist, climbs off the bed, and races down the hallway.

"Rain check on me stuffing your mouth with my dick?"

"Rain check, and for the record, you can stuff my mouth or pussy with your dick anytime."

"Duly noted. Now, we better get out there and feed the monster—and Noah," he cheekily adds. "We have a big day ahead of us today."

We're up in Lake Geneva for the weekend at our

lake house because Beau, is finally getting married to Suzanne. I'm so happy for them. Beau is the nicest guy, and Suzanne is the perfect woman for him. From all the stories I've heard about Kirby, aka Volderwhore, he definitely won the lottery with Suzanne. But in saying that, I do kind of need to thank Volderwhore, because the night Bastian and I met at Bin 501, he and Beau were celebrating his divorce, therefore, I don't entirely hate her.

After breakfast and before the chaos of the day begins, we sit out on the deck of our Lake Geneva house. Leaning back on my chair, I rub my already showing stomach and watch Bastian and Noah play together. My life is complete in every way, and now, I'm just like the heroines in the books I edit—blissfully happy and in love. Turns out, happily ever afters do happen in the real world.

And I'm living proof.

PLAYLIST

Fuck You - Lily Allen
A Bar Song - Shaboozey
Nice To Meet Ya - Niall Horan
Fly Away - Lenny Kravitz
Speakers - Sam Hunt
Nice and Slow - USHER
Can't Take My Eyes off You - Frank Valli
Riptide - Vance Joy
Slow Hands - Niall Horan
Fast Car - Tracy Chapman
Rolling in the Deep - Adele
Music For a Sushi Restaurant - Harry Styles
Under Pressure - Queen
Midnight Memories - One Direction
Torn - Natalia Imbruglia
Uptown Girl - Billy Joel
I Want It That Way - Backstreet Boys

The Zephyr Song - Red Hot Chili Peppers
Danger Zone - Kenny Loggins
Escape (The Pina Colada Song) - Rupert Holmes
What's Up? - 4 Non Blondes
The Way You Make Me Feel - Michale Jackson
Valerie - Mark Ronson feat. Amy Winehouse
Free Fallin' - Tom Petty
Accidentally in Love - Counting Crows
Without or Without You - U2
Chasing Cars - Snow Patrol
Work - Rihanna, Drake
Take Your Time - Sam Hunt
This Love - Maroon 5
Too Sweet - Hozier
Dancing All Night Through - Owen Campbell
Lucky - Jason Mraz, Colbie Caillat

The playlist can be found on Spotify.

ACKNOWLEDGMENTS

These things never get any easier and I always feel like I've forgotten someone so this is a blanket ***thank you*** to everyone that way I don't leave anyone out.

Karen Hrdlicka from **Barren Acres Editing**; thank you for everything that you do for me. You are not only my editor but you are a dear friend too.

Victoria and **Margaret,** thank you for checking all my I's are dotted, my T's are crossed, there's no extra e's or s's and repetitive words.

Raquel, thank you for the schmexy cover. This man is Bastian to a T.

Kristie from **Vanilla Lily**, thank you for the beautiful special edition cover. It's so so stunting and I'm so so in love with it.

My beta babes **Bec, Rhi Rhi, Margaret and Sarah;** I would be lost without you ladies. You give me advice when I second guess everything and you helped bring this story to life. Thank you from the bottom of my heart.

Troy, my husband, my everything. You really are

awesome at what you do and you're an even better husband and father. Love you long-time dude.

To my munchkins, **Piper** and **Kade**. You two are my greatest achievement and I'm so lucky to have you both in my life. Love you long-time guys and I look forward to the day when you are forty and can finally read my books.

And finally, **you, my reader**. Thanks for taking a chance on this holiday story. I hope you loved Bastian and Audrey as much as I do ... and keep your eyes out for Beau and Suzanne's story but SHHH, that's a secret.

Cheers,
Dana XoXoX

PUCKING LOVE SERIES

I Pucking Hate That I Love You

A Pucking Good Christmas

I Pucking Hate That You Love Me

I Pucking Hate To Love You

It's Pucking Fake

...and a few pucking more

FALLING NOVELS

These men make it hard not to fall for them

Falling for Dr. Kelly

Falling for Dr. Knight

Falling for Agent Cox

Falling for Agent Cruz

Falling: The Complete Collection

LORDS OF CRESTWOOD PREP

Co-write with Tara Lee

Thatcher

Reign

Hendrix

Saint

THE UNEXPECTED SERIES

When it comes to love, expect the unexpected

The Unexpected Gift

The Unexpected Letter

The Unexpected Package

The Unexpected Connection

The Unexpected series: The Complete Collection

THE LIQUOR CABINET SERIES

Liquor has never been so disturbingly saucy

Malt Me (Book 1)

Tequila Healing (Book 2)

Wine Not (Book 3)

The Final Shot (Book 4)

The Liquor Cabinet: Series boxset

All of these books are available on Amazon.

ABOUT THE AUTHOR

DL Gallie is from Queensland, Australia, but she's lived in many different places all over the world, including the UK and Canada. She currently resides in Central Queensland with her husband and two munchkins. She and her husband have  been together since she was sixteen, and although they drive each other crazy at times, she couldn't imagine her life without him.

Shortly after her son was born, DL began reading again. With encouragement from her husband, she picked up the pen and started writing, and now the voices in her head won't shut up.

DL enjoys listening to music, drinking white wine in the summer, red wine in the winter, and beer all year round. She's also never been known to turn down a cocktail, especially a margarita.

FACEBOOK ~ INSTAGRAM ~ BOOKBUB ~ GOODREADS
WEBSITE

dana@dlgallieauthor.com